DEAD OR ALIVE IN PURGATORY

To Robert Bedford who led me into manhood. To Trevor Siddoway, who had the misfortune to have been passed the baton, and to absent friends, who I hope to meet in purgatory one day...

When the cup that pleasure sips
Turns to wormwood on the lips
When remorse with venomed mesh
Frets and tears the writhing flesh
Fold thy wings and come to me
Sleep! Thou souls euthanasy
(From Herve-Noel Le Breton's Hymn To Sleep)

PROLOGUE

Jake Turner wasn't a happy man; it would have been fair to say that he wasn't the happiest of men at the best of times and this wet and windy Monday morning was proving to be no exception as he strode along the rain-slicked streets that led to Bounds Green underground station on the Piccadilly line.

It seemed to Jake that everything that really pissed him off would have to be endured today. First there was the rain, running off the far from adequate mini purple umbrella and onto his shoes; he'd had a choice of two that morning, a massive golf type umbrella emblazoned with the Union Jack – a "good idea at the time" impulse buy, which was about as practical as lugging around a rolled up bell tent – or the purple one, borrowed from his girlfriend which always took three or four savage attempts to lock into the open position, but could be stowed away in his pocket. This Monday morning's choice of the purple one was rapidly winding him up. Having allowed itself to be locked into place under the shelter of the porch after the first try, the damned thing had lulled him into a false sense of security by remaining upright for the first two blocks and then collapsing and refusing to stay up again. He'd had to resort to manually holding it in place and now his arm was aching, he was piss wet through and to add insult to injury, he'd skidded in a pile of dog shit, left no doubt, by some hooded wannabe gangster and his accessory pit bull. After what seemed like an age, Jake reached the station, shook the rain from the pathetic nylon canopy and grabbed a copy of the Metro from the freebie stand, before taking the escalator down into the bowels of the station. The paper was a distraction, designed to prevent him from going through the ritual of counting the stops into town. The only problem with this was, his failing eyesight, which only allowed him to read the first three or four pages before they turned into a blurry and swimming mess of print. He had given in to wearing reading glasses, but was still too stubbornly vain to put the bloody things on outside the sanctity of home. This foolish pride meant that once he'd read the first few pages, he'd have to be content with reading the bigger column headings and looking at the pictures. All this normally lasted for around three stops before he would give up altogether and revert to the default option of squinting at the carriage adverts in between counting off the interminable stops on the overhead tube map.

After a short wait, the westbound train for Heathrow, thundered out of the tunnel and moving forward on the platform, Jake prepared to jockey for a place on the overcrowded train. He managed to find a seat, but soon wished he hadn't bothered; the man he'd chosen to sit next to absolutely stank of stale sweat. This coupled with his own damp clothes and the smell of dog shit rising from his shoes, drove him back onto his feet and along the carriage where he found a space to stand and lean against the doors. He remained there for the three stops to Finsbury Park, where he was to change from the Piccadilly to the Victoria line.

Stepping down from the carriage, he crossed over to the other platform to catch his connection to his final destination. He joined the other commuters, fewer than on the Bounds Green platform, and glanced up at the arrivals screen. The next train was due in four minutes and he sat down on the graffiti-scarred wooden bench to try and read a bit more of the Metro. A couple of minutes later, his eyes gave up on him and with a sigh, he walked up to the platform's edge to try and ensure he was one of the first ones on the train and hopefully find a seat next to someone a little more fragrant than his last temporary travelling companion had been. Speaking of fragrant, he found himself looking at the thirty-something blonde in the four-inch heels, the push up bra and bottom skimming red dress. She was heavily made up and Jake smiled wryly when he saw the size of the umbrella she was holding. It certainly competed with the Union Jack bell tent he'd left at home and it had definitely kept her dry. With the sodden toes of his shoes on the yellow painted line, he looked down at the rails to see if they were out to play, and sure enough, there they were. He'd always been fascinated by the tiny mice that inhabited the tracks in between trains. Foraging for food, their shabby grey coats blended perfectly with the dusty track supports as they scurried around fearlessly until the vibrations of the next train sent them darting for cover. A distant rumble became a muted roar and a sudden swirling wind pushed along the tunnel by the nose of the train inside, heralded its imminent arrival.

Jake had been told that trains on the Victoria line were capable of operating without drivers. For this reason, they always seemed to hurtle into the station quicker than those with drivers, braking at the very last minute. This, he'd been told, was because the train's computer worked out the exact time to apply the brakes and unlike those driven by humans, had no fear of coming in too fast and overrunning. Cold hard data and electronic logic dictated speed and braking distance and they were spot on every time.

Looking down the tunnel, Jake watched as the train's headlamps appeared from out of the gloom. As usual, it did appear to be going too fast to stop. He looked into the driver's cabin, and could see somebody sitting inside. He presumed that although the train drove itself, health and safety – oh, and a strong trade union – dictated that even a train that drives itself still needed an overseer. The wind was gusting around the grimy platform now, turning the carefully coiffured tresses of the woman in the red dress, into soft whips and gluing the odd strand to the lipstick on her cupid bow lips. She stamped her high heels in a display of temper before pulling the strands free and plumping it all back into place.

He looked up to see the train's destination sign and saw *Brixton* illuminated from beneath filthy Perspex. Inexplicably, he quickly glanced down at the rails to see how long the mice were going to risk their mission and was just in time to see one last grimy tail disappear into some nook or cranny. The train was closing fast now and for a moment, Jake thought it was surely going too fast. Before this idle thought had been exchanged for another, he felt a massive shove in between his shoulder blades; the force was such, that it snapped his head back. So unaware had he been caught, that he had no chance to recover his balance. Jake Turner's last words on this earth had been 'What the fuck' before being struck by the speeding tube train. The momentum of the train, initially pinioned him to the driver's cabin, propelling him like a gored matador along the length of the platform and into the first few feet of the tunnel beyond. The impact had broken just about every bone in his body and his neck, no longer supported by vertebrae, flailed viciously against the Brixton sign, adding blood, gore and grey brain matter to it's filthy Perspex cover. Before the man in the cab had finished saying "Shit, not again" Jake's broken body had slipped beneath the carriage and lost an arm and a foot, before becoming totally entangled with the train's running gear.

CHAPTER ONE
New Arrival

Jake Turner had seen big warehouses before, but this one was gigantic – it could even have been described as infinitesimal - bigger still than the glass and steel structure that was the newly built Terminal Five at London's Heathrow airport, more vast than the ill-fated Millennium Dome, or even the exhibition centre at Earl's Court; which it positively dwarfed. Mind you, this place did have some likeness to the airport; it was similarly soulless and housed people of all shapes, sizes, colours and ages; either sitting huddled in groups or alone, each either appearing to studiously ignore the comings and goings around them, or else pacing up and down impatiently. The building had the acoustic qualities of a public swimming hall; voices and noises merged and echoed, sounding like a cross between a collective murmur and a fuggy buzz. The atmosphere felt just as stuffy as the chlorine-laden air in the swimming baths too, and its interior was so brightly lit, that Jake had difficulty seeing anything from the middle distance onwards. Anything further than that was lost in a kind of mist, which, amplified by the light, obscured whatever was beyond. It reminded Jake of the street light outside his house, which gave off a misty halo in the early morning fog. It was all very odd; he appeared not to have lost his long term memory, but had absolutely no idea what he was doing in there; he had no recollection of arriving, but felt detached and strangely unbothered about being in the colossal edifice. In fact, he actually felt quite chilled about the whole thing.

His last recollection, before arriving in this dazzlingly bright hall, was that of writing a statement in the cluttered writing room of the grimy old 1960's police station where he worked. He couldn't remember what the statement had been about, but did recall that he was writing it in addition to one, which he'd made earlier. The suits from the CID office had sent for him and requested that he cover some evidential angle he'd supposedly missed when submitting the original paperwork for the job. Jake had no idea when that had been, or what crime he'd been a witness to. Try as he may, he just couldn't recall; all he knew was, that sitting in the writing room, surrounded by the banter of his colleagues, had been his last memory before appearing in this place. He put the experience down to being in bed in his north London home, asleep and dreaming – it was obvious - what else could it be? He would wake soon – either naturally - or with an elbow in his ribs from his long suffering girlfriend, fed up with his snoring. He'd grunt and moan about not having had enough sleep, before dragging his sorry ass out of bed to go through his usual routine of washing, shaving and taking his breakfast in front of the news. Yes, he reasoned, he'd soon be awake and hitting the highway to hell that was the north circular road to his workplace in west London.

While waiting for Morpheus to release him from the bounds of fitful slumber, Turner wandered around the cavernous hall looking for some confirmation of his state of consciousness and presently came across three men dressed in camouflage. Jake recognised their dusty uniforms as being British army issue, though the camouflage was different in colour and design to that which he had worn as a young soldier back in the day. The kit he'd worn then, had been known as Disruptive Pattern Material (and in the back to front jargon of the military catalogue, it had been designated as: Temperate climate, for the use of) The DPM worn by these boys however, appeared to have been designed for a desert-like environment, and unlike Jake's black shiny boots of old, the men's footwear was a dusty light brown in colour, and of a lightweight construction. The boots fell into the category of what he and his mates used to call "desert wellies" back in his own soldiering days. Two of the men looked to be little more than teenagers, while the third, wearing the pips of a lieutenant on his shoulders, was not much older. The men were engrossed in conversation, the subject matter of which, seemed to consist more of banter than anything of substance, and sitting down on a hard wooden bench nearby, Jake began to eavesdrop. One of the younger men was speaking, addressing the man with the officer's pips:

'You fuckin' Ruperts are all the same, he railed; you just had to go on that jolly, dragging us along with you for the ride, in nothing more than a shitty soft-skinned Land Rover. Brilliant!'

The lieutenant blushed, 'Jim, you're not being fair' he protested.

'Not fuckin' fair? I'll tell you what's not fuckin' fair - me ending up as your driver and Terry the Taliban blowing the shit out of our

8

Land Rover with a few pence worth of explosive inside that vintage Soviet anti-tank mine!'

The trio fell silent and Jake took the opportunity to speak with them.

'Boys' he began, 'I was listening to what you were saying about the Taliban, were you in Afghanistan? I was in the army myself years ago, what happened out there?'

The soldiers looked Jake up and down, recognised from his bearing that he had at some point, been a serving soldier, and resisted the temptation to tell him to "fuck off and mind his own business" The officer remained sullenly silent and kept his eyes on the floor. Pat spoke first.

'What happened mate, is that me and Jim here made the mistake of going out into the desert with this fuckin' lunatic Rupert – not that we had a choice of course – when the sergeant-major says you're going with the Rupert – you're going with the fuckin' Rupert!'

Jake smiled; he well remembered *those* kind of orders, those kind of "offers you can't refuse" type of situations.

'Yeah, I get that' he smiled, 'but how did you end up here, wherever *here* is?' Pat laughed, in fact he laughed so hard, he seemed incapable of answering.

'Tell him Jim,' he said between maniacal howls of laughter. 'Tell the poor bastard!'

Jim stared straight into Jake's eyes

'What happened brother, is that me, Pat and the Rupert here, were blown to shit in our crap Land Rover and there wasn't enough left of us to fill one body bag, let alone three'

Jakes heart began to pound in his chest 'What – do you mean you're all…'

'What – dead do you mean? Yes you idiot, we're all very dead and so, my newly arrived friend, are you and every other fucker in this shit hole!'

'But…' stuttered Jake 'I can't be dead, I'm just sleeping! Now - no offence – boys, but kindly do me the favour of getting the fuck out of my nightmare!'

'You're not dreaming pal' rejoined Jim patiently, you're one of us now brother…'

'But…' spluttered Turner, 'where… what is this place?'

'What do you think *this* place is mate?' asked Jim gently. 'I couldn't tell you what this place is or where it is, but' - he joked, 'we're sure not in Kansas anymore Toto!'

Becoming steadily hysterical and beginning to doubt whether he was dreaming or sleepwalking through a lunatic asylum, the new arrival fell silent as took stock of his situation. The other soldier, Pat, his laughter replaced with solemnity, broke through Jake's meditative silence:

'Jim's right mate – right about us all being dead I mean. He isn't often right about anything, but we've been here long enough to remember what happened to us out in Afghanistan and to accept the stone cold fact that thanks to the Rupert here, we're all dead – and so' he continued, 'If we're dead my brother... what's your name friend?'

Disconsolately, looking at the floor, the new arrival offered up his name: 'Jake, he mumbled, Jake Turner'

'Well Jake Turner, if you're here in this place, here with us dead guys, then mate, I have to tell you again, that you're very much dead too. It's a bastard, I know, but there it is Jake Turner, you're as fucked as the rest of us' Cracking a smile, the young squaddie added:

'But at least you're in good company, eh Jim?'

Jake started to wail, quietly at first and then louder as the soldier's words began to sink horribly in.

'No! No! No!' He screamed petulantly. 'There's so much more I want to do with my life, this can't be it! It just can't be the end! What about my retiring to the sun, getting the fuck out of the rain, escaping the multicultural rat race, claiming my pension, going to bed when I like, getting up whenever I want to?'

The Rupert, quiet until now, stood up and approached the hysterical newcomer. Putting a sympathetic arm around Jake, he spoke calmly and slowly.

'Listen mate' he began 'I don't know what happened to you back in the world, but if you're here with us – and you obviously are – you are most definitely dead – whatever dead is. Is this place heaven? Is it hell? Or is it somewhere in between? I really can't tell you, but as far as I can recall from Sunday school, heaven is supposed to have an old man with a beard in charge, Saint Peter as his gatekeeper and a whole load of cherubic angels sitting on clouds and playing harps. Now, me and the boys' continued the Rupert, jerking his head towards Pat and Jim 'have been here for some time – whatever time is here – and I can tell you this for nothing – we've seen no angels – cherubic or otherwise, no pearly gates, no Saint Peter and definitely no Charlton Heston look-alike God types'

Jake was unashamedly sobbing now and whispered hoarsely 'Hell?'

The Rupert continued 'I once asked my mother what hell was and she described it as somewhere very hot where you would be desperate for a drink' The Rupert smiled ' *Desperate* for a drink' he emphasised 'Some kind soul, mum said, would offer you an ice cold drink and you would take the top off and put it to your mouth, but the liquid inside just wouldn't come out. Now, there's one thing I'm sure of, cold drinks are available here and the liquid most definitely comes out when poured. So, assuming my old mum was right – this isn't hell either! As for *in between*? I've absolutely no idea. They didn't cover such topics in officer training at Sandhurst!'

Jake had stopped sobbing and actually felt comforted by the young lieutenant's kind words. He didn't know how he felt, or even whether he could feel anything anymore. He was still hoping against hope that he would soon awake from this nightmare. In the words of Pink Floyd, He felt numb – comfortably numb…

CHAPTER TWO
Jake's Story

Jake Turner was dragged kicking and screaming into 1961 via the delivery suite of a hospital in Stamford Lincolnshire, this being the nearest hospital to Royal Air Force Wittering where his father was based. Born the second child of three into a RAF family, he grew up rootless, moving school every two or three years to whichever garrison town, his father was posted to at the time. In his seventh year on earth, he followed his family to the British colonial outpost of Malta.

A tiny island, measuring seventeen miles-by-nine, this was to be his new home for the duration of his father's latest posting. Malta was then, still a strategic staging post from where operations were launched to help quell insurgencies in both Cyprus and Aden (Now the Yemen). His father had been an aircraft technician working on the English Electric Lightning and the mighty V bombers of the cold war. His duties regularly took him away from the family base on Malta and it was during these absences, that Jake's mother met and fell for a wealthy and influential Maltese businessman.

One thing had led to another, and by the time Jake's father's three year posting was coming to an end, all was not rosy in the Turner household. His mother declared her undying love for the local man and Corporal Turner flew home alone, suddenly bereft of his wife and three kids. Mrs Turner and the boys remained on the island for a further six years, during which time, the romantic local man lost his money, his sense of romance and all interest in the Turner boys - now an unwanted burden. Financial hardship soon followed and they'd been left to their own devices. Jake's mother had gamely tried to feed and clothe them on their distant father's monthly alimony cheque of seventeen pounds, but even in 1970's Malta, the money just didn't cover the basics of life. Once the boys had outgrown the clothes brought from England in the early days, the family had had to rely on handouts from charitable neighbours. By now, Jake was old enough to suspect, that at least one of the pairs of trousers donated by the locals, had definitely been pre-owned by a female – the giveaway? – A zipper that was not placed in the traditional frontal position of boy's trousers, but instead ran along the side seam of the trousers he was now humiliatingly supposed to wear! Then there were the pale blue canvas deck shoes with elasticated sides, which had been so blatantly female; he'd called them his "Doris shoes!" Bizarrely – from goodness knows where - his mother had also secured a pair of Wellington boots for the young Jake to knock about in. He'd cut quite a sight in the high summer of the Mediterranean, running around in shorts and wellies while wearing no underwear! Despite the female attire and the perpetual hunger of a teenager, Jake had been endowed with the resilience of someone who didn't know any better and he'd become quite adept at scavenging food and money. He'd hit upon the idea of sneaking around the back of local bars and locating their stash of empty bottles. Pinching a couple of empties from the crates stacked up in the yard, he'd brassily gone back to the front of the bars and traded in the bottles for cash. He'd also run errands for the guys at the local petrol station in return for a few cents. Despite these ingenuities, there had been times when his belly was so empty; he'd resorted to eating food found in the street. On one occasion, his fourteen year old brother had come home and excitedly announced that he'd found some money – around twenty pounds. His mother's lover had told him to hand it over, but he was having none of it –he'd found it, it was his and he wanted to keep it! The result? He'd been thrown out of the house and told to survive on his findings. The boys had all learned a lesson that day – You got lucky, you kept it to yourself…

Jake's mother was diagnosed with terminal cancer at the young age of thirty-nine. His older (money finding, cast-out) brother had left the island a year before and at the tender age of seventeen, returned to England to take up employment. He'd left under a bit of a cloud in the form of suspicion of conspiracy to rob (himself) the story went something like this:

Jake's brother had gained employment with a petrol station, pumping gas. The takings were kept in a leather waist pouch and one of his more unsavoury acquaintances ridiculously known as *Johnny the Mushroom*, had hatched a plan with the members of an amateur gang, to rob him of the takings at the end of the night. They'd planned to confront and stab him, before stealing the money from his pouch, tying him up and leaving him in some bushes. The gang put their plan into action, but laughingly, the best implement they could come up with to stab him with was a dinner fork, with which they duly stabbed him in the arm.

Unable to obtain a work permit, Jake's brother had secured a job in London where he worked in a factory earning the princely sum of eighteen pounds a week. The tentacles of his mother's Maltese lover, however, extended the sixteen hundred and twenty miles, from sunny Malta to snowy London, and it was demanded that he contribute half of his weekly wage to the cause of the rest of the family. In reality, this meant that Jake's brother spent half of his paltry wages on food and accommodation and sent the other half, back to Malta. This enforced arrangement meant that he didn't have enough money with which to travel to work, leaving him with no choice but to wake at four in the morning to enable him to walk the seven miles to work. At the end of his shift, he'd have to walk back home again to his miserable bedsitting room. Meanwhile, the money he sent home would be added to the alimony cheque and, as far as the Turner boys could see, would be mainly spent (by the person their grandfather had nicknamed the "greasy man") on cheap wine and the rank smelling local cigarettes that he favoured. The remaining Turner brothers were pretty much left to their own devices in what was by now a left-wing country recently rid of the British colonials, and now currying favour with the likes of China and Libya's self- styled Colonel Gaddafi.

Malta still commanded a strategic position, situated as it was, in the middle of the Mediterranean, with a natural deep harbour, and China, in particular, had been very interested in investing there. Jake remembered the hordes of Chairman Mao suited Chinese, thronging the streets of the ancient capital Valletta and the dish-dash wearing Arabs – the latter openly lusting after the pretty Maltese women, unfettered as they were by headscarves and veils. In the end, the Maltese happily accepted the Chinese construction of a dockyard and the Libyan built desalination plant. Catholicism and communism however, mix with the ease of oil and water and within a few years, all was back to normal. China recalled it's Mao suits and Libya also retreated – with the exception of a radar crew left behind to man the abandoned British radar station, now set up to detect any sign of raiding NATO aircraft, should they return to pummel the north African dictator's homeland. The "on paper" departure of the lecherous Arabs left the Maltese girls to once again walk around their island unhindered, and life for the outgoing

Maltese, resumed a false air of normality. After a fairly lacklustre performance by the Labour Party, the Nationalist Party was eventually ushered back in and Malta began to look towards its traditional allies once more. As for the Turner brothers, they buried their mother on that hot rock and escaped the clutches of her former lover, passing first through a monastery – where they stayed for a few days before being repatriated to England.

As for schooling - it was assumed by the authorities, that because Malta was a catholic country - Jake must also have been of the faith, and entrance into an English catholic school had been arranged. It had been true, that during his time in Malta, Jake had been made to attend church on a daily basis. He'd even made it to the dizzy heights of altar boy; during the run up to his first holy communion however, an enlightened priest had taken him to one side and offered him something that up until then, he'd never had. He'd offered young Jake a choice – the choice of taking the final leap into Catholicism by way of communion – or not committing. Just for the hell of it, without really knowing why – but revelling in this new world of choice – he'd declined communion and so never actually converted. This was probably not the outcome that the priest - in his modern thinking, had envisaged when he'd given the altar boy the choice - but the young rebel's wishes had been respected up until his return to the country of his birth; where choice, he was to quickly discover, was no longer the prerogative of a stroppy teenager. The school had been a disaster; catering mainly for kids of Irish descent from the sink estates of the northern town he'd ended up in. Jake's new school seemed, to the recently repatriated youngster, to be something akin to bedlam. With the exception of a handful of teachers who exerted discipline, some classes appeared to have no structure at all. One particular teacher had lost control to such an extent, that the pupils brazenly lit up cigarettes in the classroom! As for an outsider such as Turner, it was get tough or die. He'd confronted some kid who'd sworn at him - (Jake had assumed that the word *cunt* was a swear word, having never before heard such a word in Malta) - only to be threatened in the washrooms later that day, by the swearing kid's friend. The boy had actually pulled a hunting knife on Jake. So much for making friends and influencing people then!

Academically, the school hadn't been much better and when the mathematics lesson came along, the maths teacher had a solution for dumb kids such as Jake. This solution not only benefitted the impatient maths teacher, but also suited his colleague who taught physical education. The deal worked thus: The kids who just couldn't seem to grasp the intricacies of logarithms, could be removed from the equation – so to speak - and the PE teacher - who made fibre-glass canoes for the school - gained an unending source of labour in the form of the young maths dunces. Mr Gladman would appear at the start of the dreaded maths lesson and remove the grateful boys from the mysterious world of calculations, depositing them in his canoe workshop at the other end of the school. There, they'd be put to work smearing sticky resin onto sections of prickly fibreglass before pressing them into the moulds that would eventually turn them into brightly coloured canoes for the school's trips away.

He'd left that school with a respect for knife wielding Irish kids, a total lack of mathematical knowledge, the underage ability to smoke cigarettes with impunity, an expert in all things canoe and very little else! Mind you - the intricacies of maths hadn't passed him by altogether – he'd become adept at spending half of his lunch money (intended by his carers to buy a healthy school meal) on five cigarettes, and the remainder on a bread roll and French fries to fill it with! He'd also learned a new word, the meaning of which, he'd innocently asked his grandmother as she'd stood at her kitchen sink, cigarette in mouth, peeling potatoes. It had gone something like this:

'Grandma?...'

'Yes sweetheart?'

'What's *cunt* mean?'

The old girl – mother to his mother - had chuckled quietly to herself and carried on preparing the evening meal.

After a spell in local authority care – there was nowhere else for them to go and the brothers were briefly fostered out before going their separate ways. This wasn't before young Jake had lost his virginity to one of the long-term residents of the children's home. At her invitation, he'd waited until lights-out and sneaked through the creaking fire doors separating the boys' wing from that of the girls. He'd crept into the room of his teenage seducer and after a bit of fumbling, he'd climbed into her bed. The girl had tut-tutted, when she had realised her latest conquest hadn't a clue what he was doing. He'd finally been guided inside the exasperated girl and frustrated her further by literally not knowing what to do next! When many years later, Jake had recounted his first sexual adventure to trusted friends, he'd admitted that he'd thought he just had to *"put it in"* and await the outcome – he hadn't known that one needed to generate a bit of movement for anything to happen – to be fair though, life in a 1960's catholic country hadn't done much to advance his sexual education!

Separated from his brothers, Jake wandered the country taking one dead end job after another; the last of which, had been a position as a grill chef in a steakhouse. One busy day, hopelessly overwhelmed by the short orders flooding in and the impatient finger tapping of the waitresses on the counter, the moody and impatient teenager had walked out of his kitchen; throwing a temper tantrum after the lunchtime soup had boiled over. All out of ideas and with no more than a basic education and the ability to build canoes, Turner had enlisted in the British Army. The army had been more than happy to welcome youngsters ignorant of slide rules and the mysteries of mathematical fractions. It had an insatiable appetite for young men to bolster the burgeoning casualty rate in the meat grinder that was 1970's Northern Ireland, and as long as you could hear, see, and had all your limbs, you were in! Jake Turner fitted the basic criteria and at the age of eighteen, he found himself part of the British Army On The Rhine, where he served an initial period of three years. Back in those cold war days, Germany was home to 55,000 troops, all poised to repel the Soviet hordes once they attempted to cross the obstacle that was the river Weser - perceived by NATO as being one of the first objectives of the Warsaw Pact troops. A fairly lacklustre non-career followed, during which young Gunner Turner set low standards and consistently failed to achieve them. He learned a thing or two about drinking and fighting in bars though and more than a little about women from the sexually liberated German girls. Oh, he also learned how to paint army vehicles until the paint was so multi layered, it fell off in brittle sheets, and he became a dab hand at sweeping roads clear of leaves – the barracks being situated inside a wood - this was practically a perpetual task. The boys, it seemed, had to be kept in gainful employment pending the Soviet invasion, and so painting anything

17

that didn't move and sweeping leaves was considered good preparation for the event. Then, on the eve of the Falklands war in 1982, he was discharged from the army having completed his contractual three years.

There had been no grand post-discharge plan and ex-Gunner Turner, quickly realising that twenty-one year olds who could fire anti-aircraft missiles, polish their boots to a high standard and wield a broom, just weren't in demand in the real world; went back to a life of unskilled and mundane employment. He'd always regretting leaving the army, but unfortunately the Falklands war had perversely served as the best recruiting sergeant the British army had taken advantage of since the bullshit "Your Country Needs You" recruiting campaigns of the First World War.

As a result of this, it would be another three years before Jake would be given as the recruiting sergeant had said, "Another bite at the cherry" So it came to pass that once more, Jake became Gunner Turner, and within a few weeks, he found himself once more back in the barracks in Dortmund, west Germany, sweeping up leaves and painting Land Rovers.

By the end of that year, Turner – now promoted to the dizzy heights of Lance-Bombardier - was temporarily relieved from sweeping and painting duties and sent off to the Falkland Islands, where he was to be second in command of a Rapier surface-to-air missile detachment, providing air defence cover for the under construction Mount Pleasant Airfield. The new airfield, being built at great expense to the British taxpayer, was to replace the outdated airport at Port Stanley and was designed to prevent any further invasion embarrassment by Argentina, whose government was desperate to get their hands on the disputed and potentially oil-rich territories. Operational tours of Northern Ireland and The United Nations contingent in Cyprus followed, and despite collecting somewhere along the way, the tag of "instant arsehole – just add alcohol," Lance Bombardier Turner was promoted to the rank of Bombardier and then, within a short space of time and to the bewilderment of his peers, he became Sergeant Turner. Eventually – and some would say inevitably – Turner began a rapid decline from popularity with the establishment (*instant arsehole* etc) and decided to call it a day. There were several reasons for this, the main ones being - the gradual realisation that he had been promoted beyond his current

capabilities, general disillusionment with the military system and –
significantly the fall of the Berlin wall. The latter, drastically, but
understandably reduced the need for NATO troops in Germany and
a comfortable lifestyle in more than adequate German married
quarters, was to be imminently exchanged for a flat in some God
awful high-rise block in south east London. His daughter would get
the chance to swap her Barbie dolls for hypodermics left in the piss
soaked lifts, and he'd get the chance to be pissed right off.

He took the decision to buy himself out of the army and in doing
so, only just pipped the Commanding officer to the post. The CO
had been about to announce a six-month tour of Northern Ireland
and once announced, he would have been committed to going.
Feeling rather pleased with himself for having thwarted the army's
latest plans for him, he had decided to remain in Germany and try to
find work. As was usual with him, he'd done no research, and as an
unqualified barely German speaking *auslander* he soon began to
reap the rewards of his impetuosity in the form of several shitty jobs.
These invariably involved hard labour and little pay (when one
particular fuckin' snake of a Slovakian boss did pay, that was) He
had found himself pretty much *persona non grata* as he'd laboured
alongside all of the other seemingly expendable immigrants such as
Bosnians, fleeing the Balkan war and newly arrived Russians from
Kazakhstan. The latter were over there claiming their birthright
courtesy of Catherine the Great, who'd taken their ancestors from
Prussia to Russia back in the day. These unfortunates – neither
Russian nor German - were hated and treated like dirt by their latter
day German employers, and for that matter, the German public. The
average west German resented the fact that, already burdened by the
new reunification tax, they were now subjected to the sudden influx
of what they considered to be scrounging pseudo Germans sucking
up welfare benefits. Jake had related to and admired the Russians
with their make do and mend attitude; they'd been used to hardship
and scarcity of food and one cold day, during his lunch break, an
ancestor from Catherine's chosen few, had shown him the best place
to pick hazelnuts. The guy – a Chernobyl survivor – had brought his
foraging skills over from Kazakhstan and easily identified the
hazelnut trees growing in the old German orchard – now a wasteland
awaiting new construction.
Years before, this overgrown orchard had given no more than the

19

capricious opportunity for laughing, rosy-cheeked German children to harvest the odd nut for fun. This same orchard now provided part of the hardy Russian's lunch, and he'd readily shared it with the hungry Englishman. Within a few months of not being paid for his labours, and literally with no money or food to eat, he'd bounced a cheque to put petrol in his old car and the ticket for the ferry from Calais in France, to Dover and then home. He'd returned to England, tail between his legs and two years of mundane jobs had followed, before he applied on a whim to Thames Valley police and yet another "bite of the cherry"

After six years of rolling around on the pavements with drunks in a scrappy, punchy "did you spill my pint?" market town; Police Constable 646 Turner transferred to the Metropolitan Police and moved to west London – an area in multicultural meltdown. Suffice to say, the work with the Met was a damn sight more varied than his last force had been, and it wasn't long before he'd become involved in a murder investigation. The murderer in question had been a certain Turkish gentleman from Green Lanes in North London – a man not used to being crossed Vis a vis his junkies being poached by a young upstart. He'd taken his revenge in the form of the time-honoured tradition of a bloody good machete frenzy. It had been a right old mess – severed limbs leaking blood and gore into the rotten floorboards of the once majestic Tudor style house, while the bearded head, hacked off before being kicked contemptuously into the corner of the cockroach-infested bedsitting room, stared glassily at the investigators. Inadvertently, PC Turner had found himself in the unenviable position of the Crown Prosecution Service's star witness.

Turner had been in the right place at the right time – or wrong time as it turned out - and had stopped the Turk in his ostentatious gold-coloured Mercedes during a routine traffic stop as he'd fled the murder scene. The Merc had flashed up on Turner's Mobile Data Terminal as being of interest to Kensington and Chelsea council, who had issued numerous parking tickets to it. He'd illuminated his blue roof lights and brought the Merc to a stop. Careless parking Mr Big had still been wearing the blood-soaked clothing from his earlier activities and after initially stopping for Turner, he'd waited until he'd got out of his patrol car and approached his window, before employing the age-old trick of flooring the powerful car and

20

speeding off, leaving Jake in a cloud of lead-free fumes. Feeling foolish, like a child, who having fallen off his bike will do anything to escape the fuss, he'd climbed back into his underpowered diesel Vauxhall Astra and headed back to the station to begin the lengthy paperwork process. There's nothing as effective as the long arm of parking enforcement and it's diligent network of Nigerian enforcers, and the authorities had eventually caught up with the Merc's owner. This had mainly been down to PC Turner's diligent noting down of the registration number (SUL1) and once two and two had been put together, officers visited his house to arrest Suleiman Muhibbi, on suspicion of the murder of his very ex-business partner. He had, of course, long since disposed of his blood-soaked clothing - a minion at the local rubbish incinerator plant had taken good care of that incriminating little detail. The evidence, although on the face of it circumstantial, had made the Turk the homicide team's prime suspect and Turner the main witness, with regard to identifying him. It had been this that had brought Jake, almost a year later, to Finsbury Park tube station and found him about to catch the train to the Old Bailey, where he was to give evidence against the driver of SUL1. Unfortunately for Jake Turner, the events of that fateful day, when he'd stopped the Merc for petty parking offences, had also brought one of SUL1's enforcers into play. The thickset, greasy-haired heavy had followed Jake from his terraced house to the platform at Bounds Green and had stood in the opposite doorway of the rattling carriage, observing his mark as he'd gazed miserably at his wet shoes. Greasy Hair, had then followed the morose policeman off the train and across to where the cop had switched tube lines. The Turkish enforcer had watched Turner from under beetle brows; his object of interest, lost in thought, was gazing at the dusty tracks and their long tailed inhabitants. The Turk had taken advantage of his quarry's reverie and with one violent shove, had ensured that star witness PC 421YT Jake Turner would give no more evidence against his master or anybody else.

CHAPTER THREE
More Questions Than Answers

Jake Turner had been sleeping – or at least he assumed he had been. He recalled unconnected thoughts – or had they been dreams? Visions still lingered, swirling around in his head. Black and white scenes of him sitting on a sun drenched rock holding a homemade fishing rod with a person he knew to be his mother, competed disjointedly with vivid Technicolor frames of marching soldiers, Bosnian bricklayers and flashing blue police lights. All of these dreams and visions, whatever the hell they were, had been punctuated with the raucous and brain piercing sound of sirens. He looked around him, if this was a dream, it was proving to be a long one; and unlike the customary awaking from a jumbled nightmare, with mercifully only a blurred recollection, the continuity of it remained. The echoing warehouse still looked the same and the various groups and individuals appeared not to have moved. Hearing a commotion behind him, he turned to see two of the soldiers he'd met earlier, rolling around on the floor trading blows. The one he knew as Pat was standing over the lieutenant and Jim, who were going at it hammer and tongs. Pat cheered his fellow Private on, encouraging him to "kick the fuck out of the Rupert" Assuming the Privates still blamed the officer for their untimely demise, Jake turned his back on the melee and tried to make some sense of what had happened to him.

His short-term memory was still eluding him and although the soldiers had earlier emphatically informed him that he was dead, he still firmly believed that he was cruelly locked in a state of dreaming and that at any moment he would awake from this land of the dead and return to the police station writing room and his statement. Getting up from his bench, he wandered around looking for goodness only knew what. He began to pace up and down and was presently joined by a young man with a shock of flame red hair who looked strangely familiar - familiar in a "looking at old photographs on Face book kind of familiar" Then suddenly it hit him – 'Lenny?! Lenny Roberts?! Christ on a bike!' He was feeling scared now, shitting himself, if the truth be known; he may have been a lacking on short term memory, but there was no mistaking the fact that

22

dream or not, Lenny Roberts was most definitely standing right before his very eyes.

Lenny had been what he didn't mind calling his best friend back in the early 80's and during Jake's first bite of the cherry. They'd misspent their youth together in the German garrison town of Dortmund, drinking their way through a small brewery and generally raising hell. He remembered going most Sundays with Lenny to the seedy part of town to get their clothes washed at the coin operated Laundromat just behind the state regulated brothel in Linien Strasse. They'd put their clothes into the washing machine and while they waited for the wash cycle to complete, Lenny would always insist that they "went to see the girls" – the girls being the whores who plied their trade in the little cul-de-sac close by. The girls to whom Lenny had referred, occupied tiny studio flats, the front windows of which, they would sit in, dressed in their regalia of stockings, suspenders, peek-a-boo bras and frilly panties. They'd sit there in all their pornographic glory, enticing "window shoppers" in with promises of a good time. Window shoppers would wend their lascivious way, along the narrow street starting down at the cheap end, where straightforward quickies cost twenty Deutschmarks, and then gradually progress along the cul-de-sac of glorious filth, increasing as it did in price, time allowed, and lurid sexual promises. Legend had it – although, Lenny and Jake had never quite had the courage to confirm it – that at the very end of the street, stood the "Whipping House", where all twisted fantasies could be realised. This part of the street was said to house sadistic creatures, which for a price would whip you into submission. The Whipping House, was also said to contain a room where perverts could lay underneath glass tables and get off to the sight of a lady of the night astride the table, defecating!

Lenny had loved his cars and Jake remembered how proud he'd been when he'd bought the red Mini with the black vinyl roof. Lenny had cherished that car and washed and polished it until it had gleamed like new. He'd driven it onto the ferry at the Belgian port of Zeebrugge, disembarking four hours later at Dover, before driving it to the Royal Artillery training school at Larkhill in Wiltshire, close to the enigmatic stone circles of Stonehenge. Jake's friend had gone there on a gunnery course, and on one particular night off, had driven his pride and joy into the nearest village with a fellow student to enjoy some downtime. Later that night, on their way back to camp, Lenny had misjudged a bend on an unlit country road and careered off the road and into a ditch. The Mini had impacted with a tree with such force that it had killed Lenny instantly. His passenger had been thrown clear and managed to crawl some distance before lapsing into unconsciousness. He'd died from exposure some hours later, the car having been hidden from view until found by a farmer late the following morning. Lenny's untimely death had affected Jake in a big way and the last time he'd seen his friend, was at the wake held at Lenny's mother's house. Jake had reluctantly approached the open casket and taken one last look at his friend and soul-mate as he lay there his face the colour of chalk, surrounded by white gathered silk; seemingly at peace, before accompanying him to the cemetery, where along with friends and family, he'd acted as coffin bearer. Looking at his friend now, in this place, it struck Jake, that his old mate looked just as he had all those years ago in Germany. How could this be? He knew for a fact that Lenny was dead – after all, hadn't he carried his coffin?

Feeling a kind of panic rising within him, he spoke to his long dead friend.

'This has to be a dream old mate, please tell me it is? I mean I know *you're* dead, but what about me?'

His friend smiled in that sarcastic way that Jake remembered so well. He jerked his thumb in the direction of the lieutenant, Pat and Jim, now finished brawling and sitting in sullen silence.

'Jake' he began 'Those squaddies over there – I know you've spoken with them – what did they tell you?'

Jake hung his head 'They told me some bullshit about being dead, getting themselves blown up in Afghanistan' Lifting his head, Turner continued:

'That's all very fine and dandy for them Lenny, but why they should appear to me – or why *you* should appear to me, is a fuckin' mystery! Now, I've never been one to go around interpreting dreams and giving them some airy-fairy meaning – and by the way I *am* dreaming, before you say anything!'

Lenny opened his mouth to speak, but Jake hadn't finished theorising and continued, 'Like I said, you know me Len, I like to rationalise these things – I can understand dreaming about you – you form part of my past and dreams are normally about just that – past

24

and recently thought or heard about things. I will admit one thing though – I am puzzled by everyone I've seen here so far – apart from you. I can honestly say, I've never seen *any* of them, *ever!*'

Lenny waited patiently for his old friend to finish his soliloquy before gently taking hold of his arm. 'What else did those squaddies tell you mate?' he asked softly.

His friend looked down at the floor again. 'They told me that they were dead' he repeated quietly. 'They added that everyone here, including me, is dead'

'Jake, mate, they weren't bullshitting – me, you, them – all of us in *this place* are very much dead'

Turner's shoulders began to shake and then he started sobbing. Quietly, almost inaudibly, he spoke to his comforter. 'But, if this isn't a dream, what is it? How come I don't remember dying, where was that long tunnel towards the light and the rest of that shit? What about that whole life flashing before my eyes crap? And if I am dead, where the fuck am I and what the fuck happens next?'

'The truth is Jakey, I can't really explain, you know how long I've been dead and I've been here ever since, just waiting. Like you said, it's just like a dream, but one which never ends, one long parade of people without purpose – you remember that album we used to listen to – the lyrics described a "grand parade of lifeless packaging?" That's about what we amount to mate…'

Jake slumped onto a chair, ignoring his dead friend and the shuffling coming and going of those around him, he closed his eyes. In a trance-like state, the earlier images flashed flickeringly behind closed eyelids. The soldiers dressed in 1970's vintage combat gear continued their march through the darkness, lit up at intervals by the blue police strobe lights from the 21st century. Scruffy Russian labourers looked up at him from their backbreaking work, winking and smiling encouragement. Then almost as if some unearthly projectionist had suddenly changed reels, a London Underground tube train rattled past him at impossible speeds, disturbing the still and foetid air, almost blowing him off his feet. The shrieking sound of metal wheels grinding on metal tracks invaded his tortured mind and he felt weighed down by a living, writhing mass of fur and sinew. What seemed like a thousand filthy, grey mice crawled across his face their long tails getting into his mouth and invading his nostrils. Jake began to claw at his face, trying desperately to rid himself of the rodent invaders. Suddenly, he sat up, his body rigid and taut like the last convulsions of a death row inmate in the instant the switch is thrown on the electric chair. Then he remembered - he remembered it all, his final tube ride, and the savage shove that had propelled him onto the tracks and into the path of the speeding train to Brixton. He relived the slamming of his body into the train, his limbs being severed by the grinding steel wheels and then the merciful release from the agony of reality, the agony that was his life in that instant. Yes, he remembered, he didn't know how long ago it had happened, how long he'd been here, wherever *here* was. Was it days, months, years even? As the cruel realisation started to percolate in heart-rending drops from his subconscious to reality, he began to sob softly. The sobs became wails of anguish and self-pity. Salty tears that had been building up over many years of holding back, began to stream down his anguished face. He huddled, child-like, in a ball of misery, rocking like a lunatic. Jake Turner, late of the Metropolitan Police, cried until he felt he couldn't cry anymore, then as the tears subsided, he began to rationalise and try to accept the cruel hand that had been dealt to him. They'd been right, the squabbling soldiers from the cruel battlefield that was Afghanistan and his Laundromat companion, long since dead in a freezing cold Wiltshire ditch. Yes, they'd been right – they were dead and so was he, whatever dead was…

Minutes, here – whatever here was, seemed to stretch into hours, it seemed to Jake as though he could close his eyes and although an eternity appeared to have passed in his mind, when he opened them again, everything and everyone, would be just the same as he'd left them. There was no feeling of time passing – not in the traditional sense that he had been used to. It reminded him of the time he'd contracted a kidney infection. It had been so bad; he'd literally crawled along the floor, not knowing what to do or where to put himself to stop the excruciating pain. The doctor had been called out and had given him a shot of Pethidine, and some follow up tablets. He'd sat for hours in what could best be described as a vegetative state. The pain disappeared, and sitting motionless, he'd not felt any urge to get up, no feeling of boredom and no sense of time. He'd guessed that Pethidine being an opiate affected heroin addicts in much the same way; a feeling of the complete suspension of thought and movement accompanied by a beautiful calmness and euphoria.

He couldn't describe his current state as euphoric, but the feeling of suspension and lack of urgency to do anything felt just the same as the day of his kidney infection. Everyone here – himself included, seemed to lack any sense of purpose, belonging or identity. No rules were apparent to him and yet, he didn't feel thirst, hunger or anything else for that matter. He just *was* – no other way to describe it – Right now, Jake Turner just *was*.

'Yes' he said to nobody in particular, 'I just am'

Trying to make sense of it all in his mind, he thought about the traditional earthly stories he'd learned at school and church – stories that had depicted heaven and hell. His present surroundings didn't by any stretch of the imagination resemble any of that "keep the parishioners in line" kind of scaremongering. Bizarrely though, and despite his state of mind, he recalled a joke, long since told back in the world. It went something like this: A man dies and goes to hell. He is greeted by the devil, who shows him two different rooms full of people. The floor of the first room is ankle deep in excrement and all within are standing on their heads in it. Old Nick, a mischievous glint in his eye takes the new arrival into another room also ankle deep in excrement. The difference here though, is that the occupants of this room are standing up. The devil then asks the recently departed to make a choice of in which of the two rooms he wished to spend eternity. Although both rooms were equally disgusting, the obvious choice had to be room two, where at least the unfortunate man could stand up. Accordingly, he chose room two, went inside, and took up position. After a few minutes of him being there, a whistle blasted out, with the accompanying bellowed command of:

'Right you fuckers! Tea break over – back on your heads!'

Recalling this joke, Turner grimly thought that this may or may not be hell, but he certainly felt as though he was in the shit! 'Always in the shit' he said under his breath – 'its just the depth that varies!'

A young woman, who looked as though she carried the weight of the world upon her slight shoulders, pulled Jake from his reverie. She had approached him silently and asked whether he minded if she sat next to him. Glad of the company, he accepted her request and took in her appearance. He guessed her to be in her late twenties; she had long and tousled red hair that framed an attractive angular face. The face was adorned with emerald green eyes full of expression atop a cute button nose and full lips. Her name, she told Jake, was Sarah Tunney…

CHAPTER FOUR
Sarah's Story

On the first of June 1984 in the maternity ward of West Middlesex Hospital, west London, little Sarah Tunney was ejected from her mother's womb after nine and a half months of being almost pickled in cheap cider. She'd arrived unwanted into an alcoholic world inhabited by her mother and the stream of drop in-drop out deadbeats who serviced her. Leaving the hospital within an hour of the umbilical cord being cut, Mary Tunney had taken her little bundle of joy back to her squalid council flat via *Patel's* off licence, where, hands shaking, she'd grabbed the plastic bottle of cheap cider from the "high in alcohol, low in price" shelf, and hurried home, swigging from the bottle as she walked. Sarah's first year on earth had mercifully been that of an oblivious infant. She'd not been aware of her alcoholic mother's lifestyle and never having known anything different, she'd accepted it as normal. She hadn't known not to keep quiet when social services had been at the door on their welfare visits and had played along with her mother's game of hide and seek. 'Quick Sarah, it's the monster – hide under the stairs with mummy' It was only as she got older that her chaotic upbringing began to affect her. The endless stream of staggering men that were Mary Tunney's down and out lovers, passed her by until the night when aged five years old. One of them, left to babysit, had crept into little Sarah's room and digitally penetrated her. She hadn't told her mum – what would have been the point? She was barely compos mentis most of the time and when she did come to life, it was just a temporary rush of drunken energy, slobbering all over her daughter, alcoholic breath in her face, declaring undying love for her little princess. It wasn't to be the first time Sarah had been abused either; five years later, the crack addict who after three months, passed for her mother's long-term boyfriend, climbed into bed with her. As he climbed on top of her, his rough stubble grating her face, she'd stared fixatedly at the boy band posters on her grimy bedroom wall and just accepted that this was just the way of her world.

Mrs Tunney's little girl had unburdened herself to a school friend one day and it wasn't until she did, that she began to realise that to have your mother's boyfriend visit you in the night wasn't normal. Her friend had told her own mother about what she'd heard in the playground and in turn her friend's mother had gone to the police. It had been Sarah's fourteenth birthday when the police officers had accompanied social services to her house. Her mother had tried to ignore her daughters' rescue party on her doorstep and had refused to let them in. The social workers had spent half an hour trying to persuade Mrs Tunney through the letterbox to open the door in their wheedling, coaxing social services voices. The police officers, having already checked with the neighbours and confirmed mother and daughter were in, were impatient to get the job done and get back to the station and their bacon and eggs breakfast. They took over the letterbox one-way dialogue and were far from wheedling and coaxing. What they actually shouted to Mary Tunney was that "If she didn't open the bloody door, they'd break it down." Inside the besieged flat, Sarah's mother was steadfastly going with her customary head in the sand option and had locked her daughter into her bedroom to prevent her letting in the authorities. A loud hammering noise, followed by the thin council flat door splintering into pieces, heralded the crashing entry of half a dozen police officers kept from their breakfast. With shouts of 'POLICE!' they stampeded into the Tunney's squalid life taking the indifferent and abused Tunney junior away and into police protective custody. Later, after the paperwork, they'd handed her over to social services and sped off in their cars to the latest emergency call. By the third robbery call of the morning, they'd forgotten all about the teenager they had separated from her alcoholic mother before breakfast.

After a difficult month in an emergency foster care placement, the troubled teen had been inducted into a care home in Buckinghamshire. The temporary and well-meaning foster parents had, quite honestly been out of their depth and had had enough of their ungrateful and unruly charge. It would be fair to say that they hadn't known what they'd been letting themselves in for. Sarah had been their first foster kid and they were ill equipped to deal with such a damaged youngster. She scarcely spent a night in her bedroom; decorated in the naive way that only adults who have never had kids would design it. Pictures of ponies and fairies, a faux

French antique style dressing table and a cabin bed adorned with a *Little Miss Naughty* duvet cover. They'd lost count of how many times Sarah had had to be reported as missing to the police. Social services policy dictated that every time she climbed out of the window and disappeared into the night, she'd have to be reported missing. The police would add her to the list of all the other "missing" kids from the county's care homes and make just enough enquires to cover themselves. What the authorities didn't know, was that most nights, Sarah, having climbed out of the window, would make her way to the train station, where she'd jump the train to London Marylebone. There weren't a lot of ticket inspectors around at that time of night and should one appear, Sarah would employ the age-old trick of hiding in the toilet until the inspector had passed. Once back in London, she would head straight back to her old council estate, where she would hang out at her friend's house, whose mum would let her stay over. She may have had a miserable upbringing on that housing estate, but it was familiar ground where she could meet her old friends and hang around the shops or sit in the run down play park with the other latchkey kids. They'd sit in thin hooded tops; seemingly oblivious to the cold, sharing an illicit sickly sweet Alco pop, pilfered from *Patel's* off licence. Someone in the group would always have a small bag of cannabis bought from some shadowy, furtive Somali youth; one of the other kids would provide roll up paper and another the dried up tobacco from a mutilated cigarette. They may not have been able to spell Dioecious flowering herb and couldn't have told you the tetrahydrocannabinol content of the stinking weed they had possession of; but they were dab hands at rolling it into a spliff and inhaling without coughing, the acrid smoke into their barely developed young lungs.

Once installed into the care home, Sarah had made new friends to whose broken background, she could easily relate. She'd stopped her nocturnal flights to the train station and had begun to explore the local area with her newfound friends – and they were good at shoplifting Alco pops, and just as adept as her old friends had been at rolling joints. They were also connected with a shadowy adult network, from who there was money to be earned and new tricks to be learned. The natural law of care homes was that the inmates were drawn together from a range of backgrounds and circumstances. There were those like Sarah, who had been placed in care for their own protection – usually from an abusive or neglectful parent, and those on the fringes of criminality. The latter were usually in care as a precursor to a custodial sentence. Their parents; not necessarily bad parents, had despaired and given up on their "gone bad for no apparent reason" kids, allowing social services to step in take over in *loco parentis*. It seemed that just as prisons can become universities of crime, sadly, the same is true of local authority care homes. The staff at Sarah's care home were a mixed bunch with their own and different agendas for working there. Some - the agency staff covering sickness in particular – were motivated by the lucrative nature of the work. Those staff from the agency could almost double the wages earned by the regular staff. Others seemed to enjoy the power they exerted over their charges and then there were those who were idealistic and worked there to try and improve and educate the kids. Unfortunately, well meaning though they were, these people just didn't get the fact that the majority of their charges were beyond normal middle class parenting. This group fared the worst and was the most resented by the kids; a thirteen-year-old girl, who had been abused since she could walk, just wasn't interested in the old maxim of "if you don't finish your dinner there will be no pudding." They certainly didn't give a toss about being told to keep their elbows off the table, or being told off for leaving the table half way through the meal. So, when the kid from the council estate, used to eating pizza in front of the TV, told dear old Barbara Browne to "go and fuck herself" before storming out of the house, it should not have come as a total shock. The tragedy was, that to Ms Browne, it came as a massive shock every time it happened; although the foul insults varied from child to child, it did happen, with monotonous regularity. The staff at the care home were bound – or more accurately – hamstrung by the Children's Act 1989. This pretty much ceded all the power to the children and the kids knew it. In fact, for those who could read, the Act was available in a child friendly booklet, for them to do just that. Knowledge is power and armed with this, it wasn't any wonder that the more informed kids ran rings around the authorities. They knew fully well that if they didn't want to go to school, nobody would make them. Don't want to get out of bed all day? don't! Can't be arsed to make your bed in the morning? tidy your room? help with chores? then don't! What are they going to do - withhold your pocket money? I don't think so!

In fact, the hierarchy at Sarah's home, out of desperation to get the kids to do anything at all, had introduced incentive money. So - get up in the morning, tidy your room, help lay the dinner table, go to school, don't swear at staff - and there was a small fortune to be made!

The Children's Act also meant that the kids couldn't be physically prevented from leaving the house, even if the staff knew that they were going out and putting themselves in danger. They'd come up with the plan of locking the front door at ten pm, but those bent on doing their own thing, simply went out before ten and stayed out. Sure they'd be reported as missing to the police, but unless a patrol bumped into them, they'd not be caught and it didn't take much to outwit those making only a token effort of searching for them. It wasn't long before Sarah had befriended a like-minded girl from the home and started to accompany her on her nocturnal adventures. They'd bonded over shared their experiences of abuse at the hands of adults and had become inseparable.

It had proved to be an ill-fated union, with her friend already in the clutches of a cartel of Pakistani taxi drivers; all good Muslim boys of course and loyal to their veiled wives at home. Playing away with white infidel girls, it seemed, didn't count as adultery and they preyed accordingly on young girls such as Sarah and her friend. Starved of affection, they thrived on the men's pseudo affection and never having been called pretty before, or bought expensive gifts, they soon succumbed to the men's charms. In order to hook and reel the girls in, the men had encouraged them to experiment with crack cocaine and as most people know, addiction to this evil drug is almost instantaneous. After a couple of hits, the white trash was putty in their hands. Thereafter, the compliments and gifts ceased and were replaced by rough demands for disgusting sex – blowjobs mainly. Not content to use and abuse the girls themselves, the cartel began to farm the girls out to other drivers and takeaway workers. When they'd baulked at going down on some of the older men and recoiled at the stench from their piss stained underpants, they'd been slapped and had their crack withheld. Given the choice of suffering horrendous withdrawal symptoms and blowing the disgusting driver in his stinking cab, the hapless girls normally acquiesced.

So it went; the never-ending cycle of abuse of the young girls, let down by a system of weak legislation. In the case of some of the boys in care, known burglars had been known to pick the lads up from the home and make use of their size and fearlessness to squeeze them through small windows. Their Fagin like controllers fed them the line that as children, nothing would happen should they be caught – and they were usually right. The only people gaining from the whole rotten system were, it seemed, criminals and agency workers and the firm that charged social services fifty quid just to change a light bulb. Unwieldy health and safety legislation dictated that members of staff weren't allowed to change light bulbs.

Aged eighteen and hopelessly addicted to hard drugs, Sarah Tunney left the home and went into assisted living. This involved being given a flat within the grounds of the home and daily visits by staff who would give her tips on how to live independently, how to budget, get your laundry done and generally care for oneself. What they didn't do was tell her how to feed herself or buy washing powder, once she'd spent her weekly allowance on crack. The taxi drivers had long since tired of her and abruptly stopped her supply, cruelly mocking her desperate pleas. They'd dropped her in a heartbeat and moved on to groom the next young waif and stray from the seemingly never-ending supply of kids in care. Once the care home staff had patted themselves on the back in the mistaken belief that they had prepared young Miss Tunney for the real world, she was released from care and given a council flat on one of the rough estates in the town. She still got handouts, but these now came in the form of welfare benefits. Panic attacks and addiction had meant that she also qualified for incapacity benefit and could not therefore, be expected to find work. She spent her days and most of her nights cooped up in the tiny flat, not dissimilar to the one she'd grown up in with her mother. Talk about history repeating itself – she'd even acquired the same taste for cheap cider that her mum had. Such was her need to smoke crack, that she'd resorted to prostituting herself; bringing tricks back to the flat, where, kneeling in front of the one bar electric fire underneath the solitary bare light bulb, she'd blown a procession of men in exchange for twenty quid to buy more of the off-white rocks, she depended on so much. Sarah Tunney had hit rock bottom and she knew it. When one hot august day she tested positive on a shoplifted pregnancy test, she made a decision. Meeting her dealer, she scored three rocks of crack on credit. She'd offered him whatever sex he wanted to have with her, but the dealer didn't do crack whores. He knew she was good for the credit though and she knew what would happen if she defaulted. She was well aware of the sadistic Jamaican's methods of extracting payment – acid thrown in a girl's face was what he liked doing and an acid scarred hooker was a hooker no more.

Back at her flat, Sarah and her unborn baby smoked pipe after pipe. It took her most of the night to get through all three rocks, by which time she was little more than a zombie. As for her pregnancy - unusually for someone who slept with men for a living – she'd known exactly who the father was. Just like the taxi drivers from her time in care, the "bastard" had insinuated himself into her life. The bastard had promised her a bright future – just the two of them in their own apartment overlooking the up-and-coming development that was Brentford dock. The gentrification of the canal basin had begun a couple of years back and property developers had snapped up derelict buildings with a view to erecting posh flats to feed the burgeoning, greedy buy-to-let market. Would-be landlords, encouraged by the banks, ever more careless with their lending arrangements, were queuing up to buy second homes with a view to charging almost double their mortgage repayments in rent. The bastard had assured her, that once he'd moved up the chain of drug supply and been able to go it alone; they'd have enough money in six months to buy their dream apartment. He'd shown her just enough affection to convince the love-starved girl that his intentions were honourable, though his care hadn't extended to stopping her turning tricks. 'Think of the money love' he'd told her and while on the subject of money and the use of her body, he'd convinced her to assist with his dealing activities. He'd learned early on - had the bastard – that with the majority of cops being male, they generally didn't tend to go beyond the search of a female's handbag. Sure, the more suspicious ones would request a female officer to come and search a girl's clothing at the roadside, but even this was subject to the availability of a female patrolling in the general area. He'd been taken to the station and strip searched many a time – the cops, on occasion, had even searched him in the back of their van, but the detention of a female suspect for the purpose of a drug search was rare. To this end, the bastard – who by now had her eating out of his hand – had talked the girl into hiding Clingfilm wraps containing £20 deals inside her body. 'After all', the bastard had said laughing

'The crack heads don't give a fuck where the shit comes from – my arse or your cunt!'

She'd carried the bastard's merchandise for the best part of a year and had only once come close to being caught. She'd been well known to the police in her own right of course, but the cops had generally taken a shine to the sassy girl from the children's home. Some had been aware of the abuse she'd suffered as a kid and would usually stop and chat to her. It wasn't until the intelligence reports started to come in with regard to her association with the bastard, that the cops had changed their attitude towards her. She may have been taken in by the honeyed promises of the bastard, but she had been streetwise enough to know how to deal with the law. The time she was almost caught carrying dope, she'd been taken to the station for a search and momentarily left under the supervision of a young probationer. Playing to his inexperience, she'd convinced him that she was having her period and could she please nip into the toilet to change her sanitary towel. Not knowing any better, the green probationer, red faced and embarrassed by the very mention of menstruation, had allowed her into an empty cell, where, sitting on the stainless steel toilet, surrounded by anti-police graffiti, she got rid of the potential jail sentence from inside her. Flushing the toilet, she'd walked out of the cell and flashed the still blushing PC a winning smile. Sarah, abused by all and sundry from such a young age, hadn't been imbued with a sense of morality, but once she'd assumed wrongly, that she and the bastard had become an "item" she'd asked him to stop using her as his mule. His reply had come in the form of a stinging slap and the snarled response, that "there were plenty of other slags who would carry his shit " Truth be known, the bastard had begun to tire of the girl, who'd started to cling to his tattooed arm and show affection. He'd cruelly ditched her and ignored all her calls and pathetic text message pleas to start over. She'd appealed to his better nature, but of course, the bastard had no such thing; he'd moved on and found himself another willing and gullible accomplice. Sarah Tunney had found herself alone once more - the canal basin dream apartment becoming just that – a dream that was never going to be anything but a pocketful of promises.

Tunney may have known the father of the foetus that had taken root in her belly, but she'd never known the identity of her own father and it hadn't been until she was six years old, that her mother had given her a clue as to who may have fathered her. The little girl had been playing with her Barbie doll and was using a drawer for the doll's imaginary bed. She'd had to empty out the odds and ends inside the cheap IKEA cupboard first, and among the usual paraphernalia of odd buttons, souvenir cigarette lighters, old keys and half-used batteries, she'd unearthed a faded Polaroid photograph. The photo' showed her mother lying on a bed next to a handsome young man. Looking directly at the camera, the two had been captured for eternity in what Sarah imagined was real happiness. It appeared that they had been the only occupants of the bedroom, where, heads together, one of them had held up the instant camera and taken the snap. Scrawled in biro underneath the image on the white margin were the words "Having a laugh with soldier boy"

Sarah had asked her drink addled mother about the man in the picture, and in an unusual moment of sobriety, Mary had smiled a rare smile before enigmatically informing her daughter that the man in the photo was and always would be part of their lives. Little Sarah Tunney hadn't quite understood what that had meant, but something made her keep the photo of her mum and soldier boy with the rest of her meagre and treasured possessions. Over the years, Sarah had asked her mother, from time to time about the man in the Polaroid, but only once during the rest of her miserable life, had her mother referred to it again. Giving in to her daughter's questioning, she'd lost it and shouted that the man who'd been on the bed next to her had been a bastard – a typical squaddie bastard who'd run a mile as soon as he'd got his leg over. Then she'd cried and when the sobs had subsided, she whispered; 'He wanted nothing to do with us love, buggered off when he got me into trouble' Mary had never spoken of the man in the picture again and for her part, Sarah had never mentioned him again. She had kept the faded memory though, the one that showed her mum smiling in a way that she'd never seen before or since. She'd kept it in her bedside drawer and it had been there when her mother's lovers had breathed all over her, it had been there when she lay awake at night listening to her mother clucking for want of a drink, and it was with her now, tucked into the back pocket of her filthy jeans as she'd entered the last phase of her torrid and miserable young life. Praying for the first time, since infants

37

school assembly, she slid open the blade to the craft knife. Her trembling left hand brushing her neck, she felt for her carotid artery, and holding the craft knife in her trembling right hand, she slashed across the artery with all the strength her crack-addled body could muster. Dark arterial blood jetted across the bare living room hitting the far wall and running down onto the thin, semen stained mattress below. A blissful dark mist descended over her eyes and sinking momentarily onto her knees, she collapsed onto the floor, her pathetic body rolling instinctively into the foetal position.

A week later, alerted by a neighbour who'd tired of the sickly, cloying smell inhabiting the shared landing, the police had crashed through Sarah Tunney's flimsy front door. It was the second time they'd smashed down a door belonging to the Tunney family – the first time to take a young girl into care and away from her mother and abusers; and the second, to have her taken away to cold storage, where she'd been shovelled floppily into a stainless steel drawer of the local morgue to await a post mortem examination. An examination, which would reveal the life and death of yet another junkie let down by the system...

CHAPTER FIVE
Pass The Pethidine

Temporal punishments are suffered by some in this life only, by some after death, by some both here and hereafter, but all of them before that last and strictest judgement. But not all who suffer temporal punishments after death will come to eternal punishments, which are to follow after that judgement (The City of God 21:13 A.D. 419)

Sarah Tunney's confidant seemed visibly moved by her story and appeared to be genuine in his warmth as he put an arm around her slim shoulders. Back in the world, he had of course come into contact with many junkies – how many times had he been part of an entry team, smashing his way through the same old flimsy doors in the execution of another "tick in the box" search warrant under the Misuse of Drugs Act 1971. They had rarely found the big boys, just a lot of Sarah Tunnys – desperate addicts with at best a freshly bought score, but more often than not, nothing more incriminating than the lingering, acrid smell left by the smoke of an early morning crack pipe. Sometimes, the subjects of the search warrant had the presence of mind to hide the rock in their mouths and sometimes, the lead officer, wise to this practice, would pounce, gripping the jaws of the addicts in an attempt to prevent them swallowing the evidence. Jake had to admit, that not once had he felt sorry for the junkies, wallowing in their filth with their flats and welfare, paid for by taxpayers like him. Just like the officers that had taken little Sarah away from her mother, he had become hardened to their predicament and by the time he'd booked them into custody, written his notes and handed them on down the chain of investigation, they had joined the cesspool of long forgotten arrest figures.

He'd actually spent some time in Sarah's town – the shit hole that called itself Hounslow. The town's only claim to fame, as far as he could remember, had been its association with Dick Turpin. To his knowledge, Turpin had been a fictional highwayman, but the locals had been adamant that he and his horse Black Bess had roamed the expanse of land now known as Hounslow Heath. There hadn't been a lot of heath land left by the time he'd had the misfortune to be there; little more in fact, than a few trees and a gravel covered car park, used three times a year by the travelling fairground people to erect their school holiday fairground rides. His short stay in the run down cavalry barracks on Barrack Road Hounslow – one of the oldest army barracks in the country - had been fairly uneventful, and he'd spent no more than ten days there, during a stopover on his way to the annual army publicity tour that was designed to drum up recruits. This was known as the KAPE (Keeping the army in the public eye) tour. His regiment had despatched all the trappings designed to lure bored youngsters into the service – mobile rifle ranges, anti-tank weapons and the crème de la crème of every adolescents' dream – the tracked version of the rapier anti-aircraft missile system. Jake had sat atop the rumbling tank-like vehicle like a conquering hero and later posed next to it in his immaculately starched combat fatigues when they'd visited county shows and secondary schools. Join the army and be a man – visit strange and exotic countries, meet interesting people – and kill them! His stay in Hounslow had been dull in the extreme – not much business for the strutting squaddies there – just the odd ancient Ghurkha reminiscing over days past and the white teenage yob element from the estates of Feltham - all swaggering bravado under their skinhead hairdos. The boredom had been punctuated only by the off duty excitement of a young man making forays into the neighbouring towns of Richmond and Kingston. There he'd joined the night club queues of young bucks trying to act sober enough to get past the meathead, steroid pumped, doormen in their bomber jackets and self important earpieces. Once inside - full of overpriced lager and doused with the cheap cologne dispensed by the pushy African toilet attendants ("No splash – no gash") – he'd been free to sample the delights, and thinly veiled promises of the scantily clad, high heeled local girls, who gyrated on the darkened dance floor within.

Here though – wherever *here* was, removed as he was from the environment of uniforms, black humour and team banter, he found himself feeling very different about junkies – particularly the one he now consoled – the one he actually touched without wearing surgical gloves – the one he had an arm around, without rushing off to the police van to scrub his hands with anti bacterial gel; yes, this one, he thought, was different. Maybe he felt different towards them all now that he was in *this* place? Who could say, he'd only met this junkie; this lost looking girl with the world of hurt in her emerald green eyes. Instinctively, keeping his arm around her, he pulled her close, cuddling her. Sarah snuggled into the ex policeman's embrace and didn't think that anybody had ever displayed such genuine and comforting behaviour towards her. Sure, there had been the rare cuddles from her mother, but Sarah used to recoil from them, the stale cider on her mother's breath had disgusted her and as for the show of affection? It had always seemed mechanical, as though her mum had done it because she'd felt obliged to – not out of love, but born of what she'd perceived to be her daughter's expectation. For Jake's part, he didn't dare divulge his past employment to the girl in his arms; he didn't want to risk her breaking away from him in disgust, didn't want her to know that he'd once been part of the system that had abandoned her.

Looking around him, his surroundings were little changed since his arrival in this *place*. One thing he had noticed, was that there were no doors, no obvious entry and exit points and absolutely no clue as to how he'd appeared here – he just had. He'd appeared as though teleported – beamed down in the style of Star Trek into the perpetual bright light. The other curious thing about being *here* was that he felt no hunger, no thirst and no urge to do anything but sit around. Sit around in that odd state he'd last been in back in the world when the doctor had given him that shot of Pethidine. No ambition, no sense of urgency, no tobacco cravings or the need for the habitual earthly glass of Merlot, no feeling of need or want; he just *was*. That was the best way he had found to describe his current predicament; and not for the first time, he repeated out loud: 'I just *am.*'

Of course, he had already acknowledged the fact that he was dead whatever *dead* was, and all things considered, he didn't actually feel too bad about it. He'd often thought, back in the world, what being dead would actually be like; he'd tried to imagine the feeling of what he had called "nothingness" the state of ceasing to exist, like being asleep without dreaming, ceasing to be. He'd never managed to get his head around the concept – "Nothingness" – apart from sounding like a made up word – what did it mean? His current state couldn't be described as nothingness in the way he'd tried to imagine it, because something – albeit, unexplained, *was* going on and his existence, such as it was continued. What happened next? Where did he go – if anywhere - from here? Would he be visited by a procession of dead friends – or worse - dead enemies? What about

41

dead relatives? Would they be here too, or somewhere else? If they were here – his dead relatives – there was only one he would want to see and that was his mother, dead before he'd even left secondary school. If there was any advantage to this being dead malarkey, then this was it; the chance to see her again. Wait a minute… he thought, surely all the people who had ever died since time began couldn't all be here? Sure, this was one hell of a big place, but everyone? Jake smiled at his reference to hell and glanced down at Sarah still snuggled in his arms and gently snoring before continuing his musings…

Ok, he thought, no sign of fire and brimstone yet - whatever brimstone was. No long tailed devil type with fork in hand and no rooms with shit on the floor containing people standing on their heads. No bottles refusing to yield their contents to parched drinkers. No sign of any of the above so far – Conclusion? Probably not hell, although Jake only had his earthly beliefs to go with this on this one… So what about heaven?

No pearly gates guarded by Saint Peter? Check. No angels with long golden trumpets? Check – No naked harp-playing cherubs? Check what about wise and benign looking guys with long white hair and beards? Nope, definitely none of the above. *Ok* thought Turner, what about purgatory? The alleged place where sinners went to repent while God decided the best place to send them to. Somewhere in between heaven and hell – not particularly nice, but not too bad either, kind of like being on holiday in a normally sunny country, where it pissed down with rain for the whole fortnight and the locals waxed lyrical about how this was the worst July weather in living memory. Well, Jake had certainly experienced a few of those *"one off"* weather situations! He continued to theorise on the whole purgatory thing, and recalled some worldly situations, so uncomfortable, miserable and wretched, that whilst enduring them, he'd been almost convinced that rather than being of this world, they must surely have been of the next. *"What if we're all actually dead and *in* purgatory?"* he'd asked himself on such occasions. Was the misery part of life on earth, or part of some tedious afterlife punctuated by the odd happy event with glimmers of hope running through it? His mental list of things purgatorial had included such occasions as:

Being stuck in a car in an interminable traffic jam, on a twenty-two mile journey to work that should take forty minutes but could take up to three hours - the tedium punctuated only by traffic lights, in turn plagued by unwanted Romanian windscreen washers and with nothing but shit on the radio.

Or what about the twenty-two hour duty in the pouring rain in Westminster outside the Houses of Parliament, wearing an archaic helmet and the ubiquitous and ill-fitting yellow fluorescent jacket; his head filled with the constant chanting of some demonstration or other in what seemed to be the protest capital of the world.

When he'd found himself part of the thin blue line, surrounded by a mob baying for his blood, petrol bombs raining down during an inner-city riot.

When he'd spent a wasted day with a raging hangover or a week of the flu, sweating but shivering in his bed.

The heart-rending break up with a lover, the girl he'd loved with every breath in his body, who hadn't loved him back.

Or, when during his days as an internal security soldier, feeling the icy fear deep in his gut while leading his section past a potential bomb hidden behind some Ulster advertising hoarding; and wishing he'd been somewhere – anywhere else.

His purgatorial list had been by no means exhaustive, and he knew that someone somewhere had it worse than him. That was life wasn't it – or was it? Here though, in this *place*, he found himself smiling at the irony of it all. He may have thought he'd been in purgatory before, but where the fuck was he now? He was apparently dead, but still felt none the wiser. Doctor! Pass the Pethidine!

After a while, Sarah awoke, stifled a yawn and stretched cat-like before looking up at Jake. Rewarding his attention with the hint of a smile, she got up without a word and wandered off. He was about to call after her but stopped himself, enjoying instead the lingering warmth left behind by her body.

He wasn't alone for long though and presently, hearing someone behind him, he turned around to see Lenny Roberts, sarcastic smile still in place.

'New friend?' asked his dead brothel companion. 'You two looked very cosy, didn't want to disturb you'

Jake blushed, 'Yeah, I may be dead Lenny, but I can still pull the birds!'

Sitting down next to him, his old friend continued the banter. 'She only came over 'cos you're fresh meat, they all do that when you're new.'

'Long may it continue!' countered Turner. 'Anyway, you've been here ages, so I guess you'd know. Seriously though mate, It's all very well me accepting being dead – which I have, but I still can't work out what happens next. I mean, if you've been here all these years, does that mean I'm destined to remain here in this sterile warehouse of a place, listening to people's stories and meeting old dead friends and acquaintances for all eternity?'

'I told you Jake – I haven't got a clue – I know, because you've reminded me, that I've been dead for a long time, but until you turned up, I hadn't really been aware of time, every day almost seems like the first'

Turner sensed a change of tone, Len's teasing banter had gone and been replaced with a sadness; a puzzled and almost confused admission, that after all this time, his friend, really was none the wiser. What chance did *he* have of working it all out if Lenny hadn't?

'I'll tell you what I don't get' - rejoined Jake – 'No offence, but you weren't exactly a pretty sight that last time I saw you in that coffin, and as for me, I was pretty much strawberry jam by the time that fuckin' tube train had finished with me – so, how come we both look the same as we ever did – all limbs present and accounted for and not a whiff of dead flesh to be smelt – what are we Lenny – souls?'

This brought the smile back to Len's face. 'Well Jakey old bean; I guess we're kind of like souls, in fact, you know what? I reckon we're a couple of as-souls!'

'Hmm…' Jake mused '*Dead* assholes'

'You can say that again! But c'mon, it's not that bad here mate, we may not have a fuckin' clue where we are, what we're doing and what – if anything happens next, but at least we're not burning in hell, or passing our time in the afterlife with a load of goody goodies in heaven! And every now and then, we get to meet old mates and the odd interesting person – having said that' - he continued, in the style of Lenny of old – 'You get to meet some boring old fuckers too and they do my head in! It's not as though you can leave the place and go out for a smoke to avoid them! Mind you' – he laughed, jerking his head in the direction of the soldiers – 'it get's quite entertaining here sometimes; check them out!'

Jake followed Len's gaze to an open space on their right, to see Pat and Jim, late of the British army in Afghanistan, on their hands and knees. Standing in front of them, was a twenty-something good-looking, athletic type, dressed in gym gear. He was barking out orders to the prone squaddies:

'Adopt the push-up position and listen in to my timing,' he bellowed. 'DOWN… AND UP! DOWN… HOLD IT! HOLD IT…AND UP! SLOWLY!' Fifteen push-ups later and Adonis continued, 'ON YOUR FEET - UP!' The soldiers leapt to their feet but apparently not quickly enough.

'TOO SLOW – DOWN!'

Pat and Jim seemed to be enjoying the workout, and were responding in the way that all keen young soldiers did – the way of following orders without question; in this case, throwing themselves eagerly back down into the push-up position. Gym boy punished them with five more push-ups before barking out his next command.

'ON YOUR BACKS – SIT-UPS – BEGIN!'

'Remember that shit?' Lenny asked Jake, still laughing.

'Yes mate, I do and did you notice how in time honoured tradition, the Rupert didn't get involved? Who is that gym guy anyway?'

'That's Damien, he appeared here not long before you; I did have a quick chat with him but – like you - he was adamant he was only dreaming and not dead' Lenny snorted derisively 'I left him to it; assumed someone would bring about a moment of clarity for him at some point. He normally just wanders around alone, strutting his stuff and scowling in that "I'm better than you kind of way" Pointing at the squaddies, he continued, 'It looks like he's found someone to play with now though – the boys have obviously told the poor fucker he's not that special and *definitely* dead'

'Yeah, looks that way' smiled Jake – 'And it looks like they're paying for that unwelcome news with a damn good beasting – military style!'

CHAPTER SIX
Damien (Mens Sana in Corpore Sano)

As a spotty, skinny and bespectacled thirteen-year old kid, Damien Jones had been the butt of his schoolmate's jokes. His so-called playground buddies had cruelly dubbed him, the "Milky Bar Kid" Ironically, he'd always secretly harboured the ambition of joining the marines as a physical training instructor. Of course, he'd never told his tormentors this – he was bullied enough without imparting that information to them. Little did they know, that long impressed by his grandad's wartime exploits, he'd resolved to follow his in footsteps and join the marines. His mother's father, Ernie Bishop, had been one of the cockleshell heroes - so named, after the type of canoes in which they had been launched from the submarine HMS Tuna in December 1942. *Operation Frankton* was the name given to the daring raid planned by the marines to hit at the German U-boat operations centre in Bordeaux harbour. It was thought by Winston Churchill that such a raid would help to shorten the war by disrupting the U-boat's Atlantic patrols, thus allowing more ships from the Atlantic convoys to make it through with vital war supplies. In the event, after much heroic effort and unforeseen disaster, only two of the canoes ever made it into the harbour. Once there, the marines had managed to attach limpet mines to several enemy ships, sinking them and creating havoc among the occupying forces.

During this suicidal mission, most of the men drowned, or were captured and shot by the Nazis. Damien's grandfather had been among those captured and he'd never made it home. Ever since he had been able to walk, he'd never grown bored of hearing all about his ancestor's bravery and had greedily absorbed all there was to know about his grandad. From the moment he'd learned to read, his mother Elsie, had allowed young Damien to have the old letters, photographs and wartime newspaper clippings of the day; but most of all, his most treasured possessions had been the medals, which he never grew tired of admiring. To him, they embodied everything he aspired to be and whenever he opened up the old cigar box, which contained the musty old medals, he could have sworn he could smell the sea. His bedroom walls were adorned with recruiting posters past

46

and present, publicity photos of marines racing above the waves in their Rigid Raider patrol boats, faces smeared in camouflage cream and bristling with weapons. The framed motto of the Physical Training Corps, hung in pride of place above his bed – Mens Sana In Corpore Sano (Healthy Mind In A Healthy Body)- and he lived for the day when he'd be old enough to go to the recruiting office and enlist as a junior marine. A genetic twist of fate had cruelly shattered his dream; he didn't even make it to the training depot at Lympstone. After the burly marine recruiting sergeant had cast a disapproving but sympathetic eye over the latest wannabe recruit, he'd sent him next door to see the medical officer.

Several tests followed, which the potential marine passed with flying colours – heart, lungs, ears, and lack of piles – no obvious problems there. Next came the test he'd dreaded most of all – the eye test. The doctor had hummed and ahhd before looking into his eyes with his scope. He'd sat young Damien down and with a heavy heart, broke the news that was to shatter his boyhood dream – the lad was suffering from keratoconus, and with the patience of a benign old uncle, he had explained that basically, the boy had a collagen defect, the result of which, over time changed the cornea from it's correct and normal round shape, to cone shaped. The early symptoms of this, he'd continued, included a blurring of vision, after which, he assumed, young Damien had simply been prescribed glasses.

'In a nutshell, son' - the kindly MO had continued – 'you don't and never can, achieve the eyesight standard required by the Royal Marines. Sorry old lad…'

Devastated, the young hopeful, had left the recruiting office before bursting into tears and running home. Back in his bedroom, he'd taken down every last trace of the marines from his wall and remained in that room for two days; inconsolable and impervious to his mother's sympathy. Then, gradually, his resolve began to resurface from the disappointment and he'd made up his mind that if he couldn't be a marine, then he'd be all he could be – keratoconus or no bloody keratoconus. He'd joined the after-school gym club where he'd been taken under the wing of the surly Mr Whiteman and embarked on a nutrition and exercise regime, which over the coming months was to see him, blossom in strength, physique and confidence. To his credit, he'd taken to Whiteman's instruction and mentorship, like a duck to water. His skin began to clear up – partly due to the fact that he was now out of puberty, but also down to a change in his dietary habits instigated by Whiteman – who, it had to be said, was himself undergoing a character transplant. Gone was the curmudgeonly PE teacher of old – long since disillusioned by the lack of interest in his subject.

This lack of interest had mainly stemmed, it seemed from the emergence of the Play Station and the likes of the Big Mac replacing the traditional outdoor games and three a day fruit and veg. The current crop of school kids had long since expunged all notions he may have had at teacher training college of converting kids from the ghetto estates to a healthy diet and lifestyle and he felt more energised than he had since he could remember. After a year of totally embracing Whiteman's doctrine, spotty, skinny Damien Jones was would have been unrecognisable to his former classmates; not only had he put on twenty-eight pounds of muscle, his complexion was devoid of spots and his confidence had come on in leaps and bounds. Gone were the geeky glasses, to be replaced by contact lenses and he could comfortably run an eight- minute mile. It was with sadness that Mr Whiteman released his charge into the big wide world and his next phase of development at the local college where he had enrolled on the health and fitness course. It could have undoubtedly been said, that fitness had become Damien Jones's obsession, almost as though he was trying to compensate for his failure to join his beloved grandfather's marines. With the benefit of Whiteman's tutorship, he'd excelled in all of the disciplines taught on the course and it wasn't long before he'd left his fellow lacklustre students trailing in his wake. Qualifying with honours, he'd put together his CV and set about applying for jobs in his local area. He'd found no inspiration in the jobs offered to him in grotty leisure centres with outdated gym equipment - machinery sweated over by the grunting, farting types who wore a motley array of wife beater vests, cut off jeans and seventies cutaway running shorts. Damien had found still less to attract him in the obligatory, booming gangsta *rap* playing over the speakers, cutting through the disgusting fug of protein shake induced flatulence.

On a whim, he'd packed a bag and gone to stay with his sister in north London. It's not that he thought the streets of the capital were paved with gold, but he figured that there had to be more choice and opportunity there. Not only that, but he knew that his sister Debbie was a member at a posh gym and she'd agreed to get him a couple of guest passes. One visit to the independently run Parkside Health Club and Spa and Damien had been hooked. It was corporate and yet welcoming, expensive and exclusive without being snobby. The reception staff were airline-like in their presentation and demeanour – the females sexy in an understated way and the male staff smart and courteous without being smarmy or too chummy. No hip street talk, no saying 'cool' in that annoying way and they didn't speak in that infuriating "Australian questioning intonation" or mixture of English, bastardised by Jamaican patois so endemic in the English language of the young since the millennium.

Once inside, Damien was immediately impressed with the equipment - all up to date and in a good state of repair. There was a well-stocked weight room, devoid of grunting, spitting steroid takers and a there seemed to be a refreshing lack of poseurs. Sure, there were a couple of pretty boy types, making more use of the mirrors to preen themselves than to correct exercise technique, but they appeared to be in the minority. The majority of the gym users seemed to be composed of anything from twenty year olds all the way up to a couple of people in their seventies, all taking their fitness very seriously. 'Yep' he thought, 'This is more like it' On the last day of his free passes, Jones got chatting to one of the personal trainers. They'd got on well and upon hearing the newcomer was looking for work in the fitness sector, the trainer, who'd been impressed with Damien's level of fitness and knowledge of the industry, had told him that one of his female colleagues was about to take maternity leave. Her absence, he'd suggested, could create a temporary opportunity. The trainer had promised Damien that he would speak to the management at the club on his behalf and a week later, Jones had received a phone call inviting him to an interview.

Young Damien had impressed Naomi, the duty manageress at the Parkside Club. Not only was the fresh-faced young man's knowledge extensive, but he'd also been up to date on all the new equipment at the club such as the newly installed vibration plate. She wouldn't have admitted it to her colleagues, but the lad was pretty pleasing on the eye too! She'd signed him up on a six-month contract there and then. Damien had trailed Naomi, who left a trail of sweet perfume in her wake and click-clacking along on her high heels in her tight pencil skirt, she had given him a tour of the facilities. The fragrant Naomi had explained that the club encouraged trainers to carry out extra personal training with some gym members. Clients would be allocated to trainers, should they wish, but they also tended to generate a client base themselves. This would bring more money into the club, a percentage of which was paid to the trainer. There were certain members of gym staff, she'd said, who were content to work the floor and give the odd bit of advice or help clients with a post workout stretch. These trainers didn't tend to take on personal training and so Damien shouldn't be short of work. With a smile, she added a warning against poaching the club's clients and training them elsewhere!

Damien had seen a lot of Naomi since that first day's introduction and the manageress had been determined to get her beautifully manicured hands on the new recruit from the day he'd walked into the club. She'd flirted outrageously with him but although he'd found her attractive, he'd remained professional and responded just enough so as not to upset the equilibrium – after all, it had been early days, and he was still finding his way around, not only the club, but also around the various personalities. The Parkside's newest recruit had been happy as a pig in shit in his new role and despite displaying the arrogance of youth and a certain aloofness, it hadn't taken him long to win over staff and clients alike. His being aloof was seen by some as a challenge and the females in particular vied for the chance of being the first to penetrate the new guy's armour – they wanted to know "what made him tick" It was a bit like the wild stallion pushed away time after time by the wrangler until it became desperate to be close to him. The gym's male visitors had been in awe of his physique; built as it was, without the aid of steroids and vast quantities of whey protein and he'd soon built up an impressive client base and was normally fully booked. One morning, a couple of months into his new role, Naomi had greeted his arrival in reception; Damien had sensed that this was the day, on which he'd have to give in to the manageress's approaches. She'd called him into the office and looked at him seductively from beneath her long eyelashes. Moving in close, she'd made her long awaited move.

'I've been having trouble keeping my bottom toned'

Taking hold of his hand and placing it on her ass, she'd continued:

'What do you think Damien? Does it feel firm to you?'

He'd let her keep his hand there, against her butt cheeks, just long enough to prevent her feeling rejected, but not long enough to tempt him to stroke, fondle or grab.

Awkwardly - 'Um…it feels just fine to me Naomi – you're in great shape'

Sitting herself down on a swivel chair, the air sweetened by her scent swirling in the vortex of her movement, the randy manageress had looked up at Damien while leaning forward just enough for him to catch a glimpse of her cleavage; her breasts straining against her partially unbuttoned silk blouse. She smiled up at him and regarded him as a spider might check out its wriggling, squirming prey.

'Well… it's kind of OK, but I think, it needs some more work and a little attention…'

Damien knew just where she was going with this, but try as he might, he just couldn't find an excuse to extricate himself from the sweet smelling seductress.

'I know!' Naomi announced as though she'd only just thought of her plan – 'Why don't you stay behind after work? We'll have the place to ourselves and you can put me through my paces!'

Before the ambushed Damien could respond, she'd stood up, buttoned the top of her blouse back up and ushered him towards the door. Before he'd known what had hit him, the young trainer was out of the office under the tacit understanding that he'd be working some unexpected overtime that day, whether he wanted to or not! Come closing time, Naomi had appeared on the gym floor and - as if he could have forgotten – reminded him of their appointment. He'd stayed behind until the cleaning staff had done their thing and then gone downstairs to the pool area, where as arranged, he'd found Naomi perched on the edge of the Jacuzzi, a bottle of champagne in hand and dressed in a pink and white polka dot bikini, the bottoms of which had side fastenings tied in a simple bow. Just a gentle tug on the bows and she had been naked, her bikini swirling around in the jets of the Jacuzzi. He'd had her right there and then, a wild and frantic fuck among the bubbles and she'd clawed his back to pieces, making more noise than an alley cat. Once her needs had been fulfilled, her curiosity satisfied, Naomi had left Damien alone and had never once mentioned or referred to their after work liaison again. According to other male members of staff, this was the way of Naomi – an initiation test with a difference…

There'd been some odd characters among those he trained. Samantha for one had been a client in real need of his services. She'd been the overweight wife of a successful web designer who avidly followed all the latest fitness trends. She'd enthusiastically embraced the *Fitflops* training-shoes – marketed to supposedly tone and tighten butt and legs, not to mention combating cellulite and probably curing the common cold! She'd taken the course on the *vibro plate* under the false impression that just to stand on the vibrating machine while bobbing up and down would reduce her ample waistline, and signed up for just about every other useless "emperor's clothes" type of fad going. Of course, Damien hadn't done anything to dispel her illusions when it came to useless shoes and vibrating plates. He knew when a cause was lost and in any case, Samantha's raison d'être with regard to visiting the gym had been to unload her marital problems onto her handsome personal trainer.

There hadn't been anything odd about Rita - a drop dead gorgeous Brazilian woman in her thirties. With a body like hers, Damien had wondered why she needed his services at all – she was absolutely perfect in every way and oozed sex appeal from every pore of her olive-skinned body. Training her, he'd been hypnotised by the glory of her ass - accentuated by the tight black Lycra, which left nothing to the imagination. Equally hypnotic, were her perfect breasts, only just held in check by her bikini type top. Getting her to perform dorsal raises while he stood in front of those gently swaying breasts offering encouragement - was just about as much as he could take! Rita had booked Damien twice a week and they'd got on well. She'd told him all about her life back in Brazil, where she had grown up in the rough favelas – the shantytowns of Rio de Janeiro. The Brazilian beauty told him that as a teenager, she had escaped the depravity and poverty of a ten child, one-parent family. A drug gang, she'd said, had shot her father, after his refusal to join their enterprise. Damien hadn't divulged much about his past and certainly didn't regale her with tales of school bullying, Milky Bar Kid glasses and his rejection by the Royal Marines.

Working all the hours God sent, Rita's mother had scraped enough money together to send her eldest child to Britain on a student visa. Rita had never actually elaborated on how she still came to be in the country long after her studies had come to an end and sensing that there was more to it than met the eye, Damien hadn't pushed the issue. He was well aware of the club's policy that staff were forbidden to engage in personal relations with clients, but in Rita's case, he just couldn't help himself. He'd risked his job to go on a couple of daytime coffee dates with the Brazilian and in the process had started to become besotted with her. One day, after the Brazilian's personal training session, she'd handed her admirer a note in the style, size and shape of a British banknote. The words *Bank of England* - normally found at the top of British notes to the left of the Monarch – had been replaced in neat copper plate writing by the words *Bank of Brazil*. Underneath these words, Rita had replicated the time honoured regal commitment of: *I promise to pay the bearer on demand the sum of*... but had changed the last part to*: the sum of one good night*. Damien had given in to the enigmatic and imaginative Brazilian and arranged to meet her for a drink – alcoholic this time.

One drink had led to another and towards the end of the night; he'd given in completely to her hypnotic advances and accompanied her home to her mews cottage behind the police station in fashionable Kensington. During the tube ride to Kensington, they had not been able to keep their hands off each other; he'd spent the rattling train journey with his hands entwined around her slim brown fingers. He'd felt her firm, long legs encased in tight denim against his. She'd looked into his eyes, kissing him from time to time, closed mouthed with her sensuous lips – nothing so vulgar as French kissing in public – just the hint of a promise of things to come. When she kissed him, her breath had been sweetly neutral – no smell of chewing gum, tobacco or alcohol – just the warm sexy smell of Rita...

He'd felt on fire, an aching deep in his groin made him feel fit to burst and following the Brazilian into her cosy cottage, he had felt happier and more content than he could remember. Once inside, the personal trainer and his student gave in to what could only be described as primeval passion, peeling each other's clothes off. First to come off had been her Manolo Blahnik high-heeled shoes in the black and white Dalmatian dog-type pattern. These were closely followed by her tight Armani jeans, which she helped him remove by wriggling them seductively over her hips - she hadn't been wearing any knickers and the sight and musky smell of her was driving him crazy! She'd stopped him after that to undo his shirt, fumbling for a while, before ripping it open, the buttons flying and bouncing over the oak floorboards. Giggling, Rita had sunk to her knees and looking up at him, had slowly undone the buttons of his jeans, straining under the urgency of his manhood. Pulling them down, she placed her hands around his ass and teasingly pulled at his boxer shorts with her pearly white teeth. Damien was on fire - grabbing a handful of her silky raven hair, he pulled her closer, Rita responded by digging her nails into his ass cheeks and pulling his boxers down around his ankles. With her tongue, she gently teased him. He'd cried out: 'Stop, baby stop!' if she had carried on, he was sure it would have been all over in a second! Rita giggled again and rose to meet his lips. Keeping his lips against hers, he felt for the buttons of her blouse and undoing them, realised that his earlier suspicions had been true – she wasn't wearing a bra and now completely unfettered by man made material, her pouting breasts entranced him. Feeling Damien's stubble against her nipples, Rita groaned and kissed him more urgently than she had ever kissed anyone before, and taking him by the hand, she led him gently and seductively to her bedroom. Guiding him to the edge of her bed, she pushed him down onto the silk sheets and following him down, she straddled him, before guiding him inside her. Grabbing hold of her firm ass, Damien mirrored her urgent thrusting as, hands on his muscular chest, she rode him, her moaning becoming louder before changing into strident commands of 'Fuck me Damien – Fuck me!' Climaxing noisily, she rolled off him, dragging him on top of her. His face in her hair, he smelt the Brazilian's musky smell mixed with her heady perfume, the combination of which was completely intoxicating.

Then, suddenly and without warning, Damien felt a lancing pain deep in the centre of his chest. The sensation was like nothing he'd ever experienced before. Animal instinct told him that this was very wrong and he rolled off Rita and onto his back. Teasingly chiding him, the Brazilian asked him if he'd had enough – couldn't the gym instructor handle a Latino girl?

Had he had the breath to reply, he may have alerted her to his plight, but Damien was too focussed on the wringing pain shooting down his left arm to say or do anything. It felt just like the time, he'd touched a bare wire in his mother's cellar – like something powerful had hold of his arm and was literally wringing it out like some demonic clothes wringer of old. He felt excruciating pain in his jaw, neck and abdomen and his chest now felt as though an elephant was atop it. Rolling into a ball, his last sense on this earth had been that of smell – the intoxicating smell of Brazilian Rita - the most beautiful, sexy girl he'd ever had the fortune not to have to lick into shape. It seemed that along with his Damien Jones's childhood issue with keratoconus, the doctor at Mrs Jones's anti-natal surgery had also been neglectful in his inability to diagnose her son's congenital heart disease. Dormant for the first twenty-three years of his life, it had finally manifested itself with tragic consequences in that cosy little Kensington cottage brought on in part by the girl from the favela…

CHAPTER SEVEN
False Summits and Dog Food

Back in that place, Jake Turner decided to take a look around. Leaving didn't appear to be an option at that point in time. As he'd discovered earlier, there were no physical means of doing so as far as doors were concerned and as for leaving to go to the *next place*; if there were ever to be such an option, he thought he'd rather stay here for the time being. He had accepted that being a whole Jake Turner was far preferable to being a "strawberry jam under a tube train" Jake Turner, and yes - for the moment, being a whole Jake Turner was an infinitely better choice between the two. Whether he would look whole should he ever appear to an earthly being, he wasn't so sure. Being a sou*l* – or as Lenny Roberts had delicately put it "as-soul" – was as good as it seemed to get around here.

Strolling along the infinite space that was his new home, he secretly hoped to see the girl again – the girl who'd been the only thing akin to the warmth of life he'd experienced since his arrival. In the event, Sarah Tunney was nowhere to be seen, but seeing a group gathered around a funny looking little elderly man wearing a cloth cap, he'd stopped to see what the attraction was. He'd been just in time to hear the little guy being asked by a hefty middle-aged black woman what had brought him here. How – she had indelicately asked him – had he died?

'Well' the funny guy had begun -'Last Wednesday, I was at my local COSTCO buying a large bag of Pedigree Chum dog food as I'd decided to try the Pedigree Chum diet.'

'How does *tha*t work?' asked the incredulous woman, looking quite disgusted.

'Well' - continued the man with a sparkle in his eye - 'It's essentially a perfect diet and the way that it works is, to load your trouser pockets with Pedigree nuggets and simply eat one or two every time you feel hungry. The food is nutritionally complete and so it works well, filling you up without the calories. It does taste like shit though!'

Horrified, she asked, had he died because he'd been poisoned to death by the dog food? Looking sad, his voice trembling with emotion, the mischievous old man, drew his rapt audience in still further and explained what had brought him there.

'Oh no, it's perfectly safe to eat, but this wasn't the problem…'

Pausing for effect, the old guy knew that he now had them all in the palm of his hand and continued his story.

'Basically, having eaten my first handful of nuggets, I left the store and within a few minutes and without even thinking, stepped off a curb to sniff a poodle's ass - and a car hit me!'

Laughing like a drain through a toothless mouth, the old guy added – 'And that, my lovelies, is how I died – from a dog food diet!'

Leaving the old man's groaning audience, Jake continued his walk through the seemingly endless building. The dog food story had made him smile, but he was no further in his understanding of the world he now seemed to inhabit. There were still moments – only moments mind you – when he'd thought fancifully, that he was dreaming and that he would soon awake and go back to his old life in the multicultural experiment that had been Britain. He'd always complained about it of course, but given the choice between living out the rest of his natural life in "Londonistan" and the seemingly aching endlessness of this place, he believed he'd probably be better off embracing multicultarism. Not that it hadn't been great to catch up with his old mate Lenny you understand - and who knew which dead friend or relative would turn up next – but no, he really didn't want to be here any more. As he trudged disconsolately along the pristine floor, he began to become aware of a phenomenon he'd never noticed before; as he walked towards a group of people or individuals alike, he never seemed to get any closer to them. It was like the feeling he'd had when out tramping the Hebridean hills as a soldier; when tired out after a day's walking, he'd clear one false summit, only to be presented with another one. In the case of the people here, he'd sometimes get tantalizingly close, only for them to either appear further away, or to melt away like a desert mirage. He had the feeling of being on some endless treadmill, never seeming to gain ground.

It seemed, that something was controlling his access to people – allowing him to see and communicate with some – like Lenny, Sarah and the old comedian – but not others.

Turner sat down on one of the thousands of empty football stadium- type seats set in endless rows and presently, slipped into that merciful Pethidine-like state he'd grown accustomed to of late. He time flashed...

He was a sergeant in the British army again and carrying out an operational tour as part of the United Nations force – the thin sky-blue line allegedly keeping the Turks from overrunning the ceasefire line established at the end of hostilities after Turkey had invaded and then partitioned Northern Cyprus. He'd been stationed in what used to be a factory that had churned out orange boxes prior to the invasion. This was now situated on the buffer zone between the Greek and Turkish armies and had been made home by Jake's artillery battery for the duration of their six month tour of duty. It hadn't been a difficult posting – particularly for the senior ranks, of which Turner was one. He'd been a troop sergeant supervising administration, the posting of sentries and regular patrols within the buffer zone. He and his fellow senior ranks had converted a portakabin into a sergeant's and officer's mess, which housed a bar, a few regimental pictures, a dining area and a TV. It didn't quite match the splendour of the messes back at home, bereft as it was of ornate silver table pieces and waiter service, but it gave a sense of order, a place to associate away from the ordinary ranks. Sergeant Turner had been alone in the mess with another senior rank one night. All of the other senior NCOs and officers were away for the evening at a function and had left Turner and the other senior NCO to mind the shop and take care of the men as they carried out guard duty and mobile patrols of the buffer zone patrol track. He'd had problems back at home in Germany with a troublesome and unfaithful wife who, not content with her infidelity, had taken to spending his money like water - needless to say, this had been a difficult period of his life. He'd been on a session and taken on vast quantities of the local beer, followed by chasers, and after a few hours of this, began inexplicably to smash up the mess building. He'd smashed all the regimental pictures, thrown bottles and glasses onto the floor and then, for good measure booted the TV off the table. His fellow senior NCO – an ex-submariner of some repute within the regiment, had been totally taken aback by the latest manifestation of "instant arsehole – just add alcohol" and simply roared with laughter! At one point in the proceedings, a junior NCO

58

who'd been leading a mobile patrol, burst in upon the carnage. He seemed visibly upset and after incredulously surveying the wreckage that had once been an orderly sergeant's and officer's mess, blurted out, that a Turkish soldier had just taken a pot shot at his patrol. Unfortunately, the hapless NCO was greeted with a "So fuckin' what?' from the instant arsehole, that was his immediate superior and he left the mess thinking that the lunatics had taken over the asylum.

Later that night, when the grown-ups returned from their function, they were greeted at the entrance to the camp, by the sight of a very drunk senior NCO sitting in an old, but still functioning Turkish minefield, resisting all the efforts of the disapproving corporal guard commander, exhorting him to return to safety. Eventually, the officers persuaded Turner to go to bed and the next morning, woken by the still laughing submariner, he was taken to inspect the ruins of the sergeant's mess. Embarrassed, with a splitting head and uncomprehending of his nocturnal activities, he'd been hauled before the battery commander – who himself had been a bit of a character with a colourful past and the horrors of the Falklands war behind him. Luckily for the disgraced senior NCO, the BC had empathized with the alcohol driven antics of his subordinate and decided on the lenient sentence of banishment to another UN outpost, where he'd served out the rest of the tour in relative sobriety.

Coming out of his Pethedine reverie, Jake wondered whether *this place* was where he was to be confronted by the demons of his misdemeanours past. He thought wryly, that if that were to be the case, it was going to be one long bastard of an afterlife…

Deep in thought and reflecting on his past wrongdoings, Turner hadn't noticed the funny dog food-eating guy who had shuffled up and sat himself down in the chair opposite, until he heard him coughing theatrically. "Harry" - he'd said his name was – whether Jake was remotely interested was of no consequence to the man. 'Harry Thomas' he added, extending a gnarled hand. Disinterestedly, Jake took the proffered hand. 'Jake - Jake Turner' he managed. 'What brings you here?'

'What – apart from being dead?' cackled the old man. 'You *are* dead too, I assume?'

'Apparently so, how long have you been here Harry?'

His rheumy old eyes twinkling, Thomas spread his hands. 'How long is a piece of string? I know that I reached the grand old age of seventy-six, because I can remember that particular birthday, so I can't have been here all that long. You know how it is here though Jake – time is a thing of the past. To be honest, I really don't have a clue – I just…' Harry trailed off.

'You just *are*?' completed Turner. He'd phrased it more in the way of a statement than a question, recalling his own version of their current position. Harry liked this.

'That's exactly right my boy – couldn't have put it better myself!'

Slapping himself on the thigh, he reveled in this eureka moment. 'Yes Jake Turner – we just *are*!'

Harry was looking intently at Jake now, making him feel uneasy, then the old guy dropped it on him; 'Kif inti Jakey?'

Those three words startled Turner – he hadn't been asked how he was in the Maltese language for a very long time – not since he'd fled that island after his mother's death in fact. As for being called *Jakey,* that wasn't a term of endearment commonly known outside his intimate circle. His mind raced and he stared at Thomas, his brain swirling with kaleidoscopic images of a time and place a million miles away. His wrinkled old face wreathed in smiles, Harry teased him:

'First met you when you were a freckly five year old whippersnapper back on Hot Rock'

There he went again! Trotting out another colloquialism Jake hadn't heard for the longest time – "Hot Rock" – the local's pet name for Malta. 'OK, I'll play your silly game old timer – hit me with another clue'

Thomas was enjoying himself. 'How's that scar on your right foot Jakey?'

Turner reached down instinctively to his foot. He had been the owner of a jagged one inch scar on the top of his foot since he'd been five or six years old. This had been the result of winding up his stressed out mother one evening. She'd been at the end of her tether with marital problems and three pain in the ass kids weren't helping. The last straw had come when young Jake had wandered into the kitchen with his dinner plate and petulantly announced that he wasn't going to "Eat this bloody crap" (The words bloody and crap had been the latest profanities he'd learned from one of the older boys at school)

His mum had gone ballistic and in her frustration had hurled the glass jar she'd been holding, with all her frustrated might onto the tiled floor. Unfortunately, she'd misjudged her aim and had hit Jake on the foot with it. The jar had smashed on his foot, the result of which was blood all over the white tiles and one very sorry mum! She'd run outside and flagged down his dad, who was driving back from work. Frantically signaling for him to turn the car around, she'd bundled the wounded boy into the car and they'd sped off to the air force base, from whence his dad had just come. They'd taken him into the camp sick bay, where he'd been stitched up (rather badly) by the medic corporal who'd been a friend of his father.

What had he been called again? Corporal... Thomas! Shit! Corporal Harry Thomas – late of Her Majesty's Royal Medical Corps! That was when the penny dropped – he could see him now, reflected in the wizened old face opposite him. He could just about recognise the features of what had once been the gregarious, good-looking guy. He remembered the bushy mane of dark wavy hair, brushed back and Brylcreemed, which gave him a look not unlike that of a young Elvis Presley. Jake recalled the twinkling eyes and the ready smile that had captivated the girls – his mum among them - and he could hear the big larger than life laugh. Cpl Thomas, the life and soul of the party had always been around; the beach barbeques, house parties, you name it, if there was alcohol to be had, he was your man. He'd been a permanent fixture in the beer tent on camp open days and Jake had heard it said that Harry Thomas would turn up to the opening of an envelope! He drank like a dog in the sun and had been affectionately known as *"Dog"* and up until his father had left the island; Harry always seemed to have been around during those first few years of Jake's life. The two deceased men stood up and hugged each other. Jake laughed, and held up his foot for inspection.

'You mean *this* scar? A right fuckin' mess you made of stitching me up that day Dog; come to think of it, it looks like a bloody dog's hind leg too! – Mind you, you'd probably been on the beer before dad brought me in!'

The old medic laughed in that Harry kind of way that Jake remembered from all those years ago. Cuffing him lightly on the ear he countered: 'You always were a cheeky little bastard! That was craftsmanship that sewing-up job!'

It was at one of RAF Luqa's summer balls, that Harry had first met Jake's father; and they'd become close friends. Every now and then, the young Turner brothers had been entrusted into his care for the evening. The boys always looked forward to the *Dog* babysitting them. He normally came bearing gifts and had somewhere along the line, learned a couple of magic tricks with which he entertained them. Their favourite was the one when he seemed to pull a shilling coin out of thin air from behind their heads – favourite because they got to keep the coin after the trick! Harry used to let them drink a small glass of his *Hop Leaf* beer too - not that they liked the bitter taste, but to his amusement, they'd always feigned manly enjoyment before going to bed, their little heads spinning! If he'd been honest, he would have admitted to Jake, that yes; when he'd sewn up the boy's maternally inflicted foot wound all those years ago – he *had* still been under the alcoholic influence from some party or other the night before! They sat in silence then, the old corporal and the policeman, both lost in thought, transported once more to those carefree days on Hot Rock…

CHAPTER EIGHT
Harry's Story

The year 1935 saw the births of Elvis Presley, Woody Allen, Luciano Pavarotti and the Dalai Lama. This was the same year Amelia Earhart flew solo across the Pacific, Alcoholics Anonymous was founded in New York - and ironically, the first canned beer went on sale. It was also the year that Harold Frederick Thomas took his first breath.

Born to Ethel and Earnest Thomas, he began life in the West Midlands Black Country town of Willenhall, historically famous, for the manufacture of locks and keys. (As early as 1770, Willenhall was home to one hundred and forty eight locksmiths) Harry's parents both worked at the Chubb lock-making firm - Ethel in the canteen and Earnest on the shop floor. Earnest, along with the hundreds of other workers, who'd started work in the industry at the age of fourteen, developed in later years a hump on his back. This unfortunate phenomenon was as a result of sixteen-hour days, bent almost double over the lock making benches, before their young bodies were fully developed, and Willenhall had been given the affectionate nickname of "Humpshire" So prevalent had the condition been, that some local public houses had actually made holes in the wall behind the wooden drinking benches to more comfortably accommodate their patrons! The Bell Inn, where Harry's father used to drink, leaving the boy outside on the cold step' still had the hump holes as late as the 1950's.

Earnest had been a strict father, and misdemeanours such as reaching across the dinner table for the salt pot, would earn Harry a rap across the back of the hand delivered by means of the cane he kept next to the table for such transgressions. It wouldn't have been too far from the truth, to say that young Harry had been an unloved child – not ill-treated, but definitely a victim of the Victorian adage that "children should be seen and not heard" This hadn't been helped by the fact that Ethel had come home one day unexpectedly, to find Earnest in bed with one of the factory girls. Divorce hadn't been an option back then and so Harry's parents had remained together, while living separate lives. The boy had spent as little time as possible at home and had found refuge at the local Air Cadet group. He'd never been allowed to bring school friends home for tea, or to associate with anyone outside of school hours and his early childhood days had been lonely. As a teenager in those austere days of post-war Britain, he'd been befriended by one of the masters at his school. The Geography teacher had flown Sopwith Camels during the First World War, and complete with bristling handlebar moustache, the old boy had made quite an impression on the boys. In his spare time, the veteran pilot ran the local air cadet detachment and having recognized Harry's perpetual air of sadness, he'd encouraged the boy to come along to the airfield. Endowed with a newfound zest for life, he'd enjoyed adventure and friendship with the cadets, and when away with them, had enjoyed three square meals a day. He'd even been able to fly in the Royal Air Force gliders, breaking free of the earthly bonds that confined him in the strict and miserable house below. By the age of sixteen, Cadet Thomas had accomplished a solo flight and it hadn't been long, before with the indifferent permission of his father, he had enlisted in the RAF as a boy entrant.

His local training centre had been RAF Hednesford in Cannock Chase and at number 11 school of recruit training; he'd spent eight weeks basic airman training. Among the thrills of being trained at Hednesford, were the two operational Spitfires still stationed at the base. He was in awe of these legendary war birds and the sound of their mighty Merlin engines on full song had thrilled him to the core. Had he not been deemed unfit for flying duties by his colour blindness, he would have joined the other hopefuls on pilot selection. As it was, he opted for medical training, reasoning that at least this would be a transferrable skill should he ever leave the RAF. Back then, Aircraftsman Thomas's nearest RAF medical training centre was at RAF Freckleton on the Wharton aerodrome, located between Preston and Blackpool in the north west of England. This was to be Harry's first trip away from his hometown and with free time being spent in the holiday resort of Blackpool, he'd grown up fast and acquired a taste for alcohol, girls and partying.

Once out of training, he'd been more fortunate than his National service buddies, in that he'd had more of a choice of where he wanted to be posted. Malta sounded pretty exotic to him - and as a couple of his drinking buddies were already based there - Malta it was. The island's new post-war airfield - RAF Luqa - was the current home to 39 squadron, which was equipped with Gloster Meteor night fighters, and freshly promoted Lance-Corporal Thomas was soon ensconced in the newly built medical centre. By day he dealt with the triaging of airmen reporting sick. Some of them obvious malingerers (so called bad backs topped the list), some with coughs and sneezes and those who'd spent too much time and money in the capital's red light district in Strait Street. There, down in *The Gut,* the men picked up all manner of weird and wonderful ailments. Contracting venereal disease – colloquially known as the pox, a dose, the clap or a blobby knob, was practically *de rigueur* among the Gut's clientele. Of course, the nature of such an infection often meant that the men were too shy and ashamed to seek medical help until the disease was advanced. Worse than the fear of humiliation was the military myth, that when you reported sick with VD, the medical officer would carry out the following ghastly procedure: An instrument described as an umbrella would be inserted into the sufferer's urethra, and once inside it would be opened umbrella-style. Apparently – or so the old sweats would say - the next process involved the slow and agonising withdrawal of the opened umbrella, scraping away the infection as it went. This nightmarish but mythical story for the treatment of a blobby knob, along with stationing military padres outside houses of ill repute; was all part of the authorities' efforts to steer the fighting men clear of such establishments. Of course, this had little or no effect on the young and virile servicemen, and Cpl Thomas was kept busy with a steady stream of victims of the Gut. Not that he did anything to refute the myth of the umbrella; in fact, with classic military black humour, he had kept one of those miniature, paper cocktail umbrellas in his drawer for such occasions. Once the unfortunate airman had confided in the medic, Harry would open the drawer and take out the cocktail decoration. Much to the horror of the patient, he would then slowly and deliberately open the umbrella, while grimacing and inhaling noisily through his teeth in an all too obvious depiction of pain. His cruel perpetuation of the umbrella myth complete, he'd then send the by now terrified sufferer on the long walk down the long narrow corridor to the medical officer's surgery.

Harry had never felt the need to risk getting a dose down in Strait Street; inundated, as the handsome medic had been, by offers from members of the base WRAF – the women's branch of the Royal Air Force. Unfortunately for Thomas however, his taste in women wasn't confined to the WRAF girls and after a chance meeting with the flirtatious wife of the station commander, he - a lowly junior NCO embarked on a fateful affair with the wife of a Group Captain. She'd arrived at the guardroom early one summer's evening when Cpl Thomas had been guard commander. Harry wasn't normally required to carry out guard duty, but most of the station – the commander included – had been drafted in to help in the worsening situation in the Southern Arabian Protectorate of Aden (now Yemen) and due to the shortage of manpower on the base, Harry had been required to perform the duty of guard commander on a day-on-day- off basis.

Phyllida Parker-Jones had appeared at the guardroom dressed in a flimsy floral patterned dress that clung seductively to her curvaceous body. Her honey blonde hair was tied back in a silky ponytail and she wore just a trace of makeup on her oval face. Harry had seen her around the base before, but reasoning that being the wife of the station commander – aka God – he'd reasoned that she was well and truly out of bounds.

Looking at the guard commander in that way somewhere between the haughtiness of privilege and the flirtatiousness of a woman bent on getting her way, she informed the very attentive corporal, that there was an electrical fault in the station commander's house to the effect that she had no electricity at all. She'd said something disparaging about the standard of work displayed by the local electricians who'd not long left the house having rewired the kitchen. Could he, the guard commander help? Now, it could never have been said that the Dog was shy around women, but this one was different. This one, was the wife of a Group Captain, the station boss - her wish was his command - and he'd not been about to fob her off whatever his lack of electrical knowledge had been. Whether it had been her husband's lofty position, or the fact that she exuded sex from every inch of her curvy body, he didn't know; but before he knew it, he was telling the guard second-in-command to mind the fort until he got back. Grabbing a flashlight from the back room, he'd followed that mesmerising ass as she walked, her hips swaying and heels click-clacking on the pavement towards the home of the station commander and his wife. What an ass! He'd thought it looked like two soft-boiled eggs inside a silk handkerchief! 'Steady Dog' he thought admonishingly – 'She may have a great ass, but it's the ass of a high ranking officer and saluting it is as close as you'll ever get!'

Following the glory of that ass along the path to her house, his nostrils were filled with the sweet smell of the ubiquitous fig trees that lined their route. Heated by the day's Mediterranean sun, their rich smell competed with the delicate yet intoxicating perfume of the white jasmine flowers in the station commander's courtyard. Phyllida Parker-Jones let them into the house, darkened by the heavy wooden shutters designed to keep the fierce midday sun out. The Dog wondered momentarily why she hadn't opened the shutters to allow the last of the failing light through to aid their progress into the cool interior, but nonetheless, complied with her instruction to switch on his flashlight. He wasn't about to ask why the silly moo hadn't opened her shutters – after all – he was the corporal and she was the boss's wife! They'd continued into the house, the flashlight creating eerily dancing shadows out of the furniture. The fuse-box, she'd informed him, was in the cellar and following the yellow beam of the guardroom torch, they'd opened the creaking door to the cellar. Telling him to watch out for the steep steps, she followed him as he'd descended into the cool musty basement.

Locating the fuse-box behind some packing cases, Harry turned off the mains power switch and began to extract the fuses one by one, examining them for the telltale broken wire that would explain the lack of power in the house. Pulling out the third one, he shone the torchlight on it to reveal the culprit and removing the burned out wire bridge, he replaced it from the roll of fuse wire on top of the box, disturbing a hidden gecko as he did so. Seeing the reptile scurry off into the darkness, Phyllida gave a little squeal. Dog mused that this was very unlike the "jolly hockey sticks" officer's wife kind of a woman, he'd assumed her to be.

Shuddering, she'd giggled, 'I hate those damn things!'

He sensed, rather than heard the woman moving closer behind him. Snapping the Bakelite fuse back into place, he was about to throw the mains switch back on, when he felt her arms around him, her manicured hands snaking inside his khaki uniform shirt, stroking the hair on his chest. Taken aback, the corporal had begun to protest;

'Ma'am?' he managed to splutter, before she put her lips to his ear. 'Sshh…' she hissed, her sweet hot breath on his face, and as she did, Phyllida, wife of the station commander, moved in even closer. Harry could feel her pelvic mound gently pushing into his backside; he felt those amazing breasts below his shoulder blades and her firm thighs against the back of his legs. Thinking "fuck it" he reached behind him and grabbed hold of that divine ass and pulled her further into him. Groaning, she cooed 'Mmm… now, that's nice!'

Turning around to face her, he gently took hold of her face, cupping it in his hands before kissing her – tenderly at first, then with a hunger he'd not known before. She kissed him back, nibbling on his bottom lip while her hands grabbed urgently at his ass pulling him tightly against her while thrusting her hips deep into him. He ached for her – a deep animalistic ache – an ache that urgently demanded a release. Christ! He wanted her so badly! For her part, Phyllida was on fire; she'd grown so used to the drunken fumblings of her husband - the out of duty monthly servicing of the little woman on his return from some official function or another – one more chore to be ticked off on the list of a top ranking officer with an operational airbase to run and a lot on his mind.

Unzipping her dress, he tugged it down over her perfect upturned breasts, past her guitar hips and down to her pretty feet, which he lifted one at a time, finally freeing her of her floral patterned modesty. Then, gently taking her nipples between his teeth, he tugged at them, making the horny station commander's wife emit little gasps of pleasure. Continuing his exploration of that horny body, Harry planted kisses down the length of it, lingering briefly just above the sweet smelling thatch of pubic hair before entering her with his tongue. Groaning, the officer's wife grasped her lover's head tightly, pulling him ever closer and enveloping his head within her creamy thighs. Pulling her down onto the dusty concrete floor, Harry took her, right then and there in the musty darkness of the cellar in the house of the station commander. He couldn't remember ever having been so desperate to have a woman before and climaxing noisily together, they lay in the dust panting and holding each other close.

He didn't know how long they had lain there in the dust, but reality and the enormity of what they had just done began to kick in when he heard a member of the guard doing his rounds somewhere above him in the now totally dark garden. Phyllida seemed oblivious to the reality of their illicit liaison and protested when Harry disentangled himself from her and began to fumble around for his uniform, scattered somewhere on the cellar floor. Eventually finding his clothing, discarded in the throes of passion, he retrieved Phyllida's dress from the top of a packing case and passed it to her. She was having none of it though and tossing it away from her, she grabbed his flashlight and made her way over to the fuse-box in the corner. Once there, she deftly threw the mains switch like a pro, bathing her glorious nudity in the glow of the dim ceiling light.

'Darling' she purred 'Were you really taken in by my damsel in distress routine? I've been watching you, Corporal Harry Thomas and I've been desperate to get my hands on you ever since you booked me in for my inoculations! Well? What do you think about that?'

Harry didn't quite know what he thought about this revelation, but he did know that if he didn't get his ass back down to the guardroom soon, they'd be wondering what had become of him.

'Well?' she repeated pushily, walking towards him, her hips swaying, lips pouting – 'You've not gone all shy on me have you, my clever fixer of fuses?'

If he was honest, Harry's desire, his urgent lusting after Miss Posh Knickers, had flooded out of him at the point of orgasm, taking his confidence with it. As he'd followed the station commander's wife along the path to her house, he'd fantasised about having her. Never in a million years, had he expected to have been fucking the ass off her in the cellar; but now that he had – well – he felt that empty, "just had a casual non-relationship fuck" type of feeling – the one that says "well that was good – can't be bothered with the pleasantries, just want to get the fuck out of here now!"

Suddenly feeling ridiculous in his nakedness, he spluttered something inane about having to get back to keeping the camp safe, hurriedly threw on his crumpled uniform and fled. Giggling, Phyllida called out after him. 'Don't be a stranger Corporal Thomas!' Walking back to the guardroom, Harry could smell her musk on him. The awful realisation of what he'd done began to dawn on him. 'Another fine mess you've got me into' he muttered glancing down at the source of his predicament. 'You just couldn't keep it in your pants could you Thomas? For fuck's sake, what a mess!'

He'd tried to go back to his uncomplicated NCO life; beers with the boys in the junior ranks club, guard duty and joking around with the WRAF girls, but deep down, he knew things would never be the same again for him at RAF Luqa and he was right. Two weeks after his cellar liaison with the boss's wife, he had been in his cubbyhole of an office in the medical centre, when in she came. She arrived airily on a wave of Chanel, all tits and teeth.

'I think you've been avoiding me corporal Thomas,' she teased. 'So' she continued, enjoying the barely concealed look of horror on his face. 'If Mohammed won't come to the mountain...'

Laying a hand on his starched white medical tunic, she dropped a prettily wrapped package onto his desk.

'Just a little something to keep you warm at night...' and then she was gone, that amazing ass swaying atop her high-heeled boots. It wasn't until after she'd departed that he realised he hadn't said a single word during her brief visit. In fact, he was pretty sure that he'd done a pretty good impression of catching flies as he'd opened and closed his mouth in the manner of a beached trout. He'd had to admit, that despite his misgivings on that fateful evening as he'd fled the scene of the crime, her very presence made him feel horny as hell! Closing his office door, he unwrapped the heavily scented package to reveal a pair of lacy French panties a door key and an immaculately written note in the form of a poem:

Harry, Harry, oh Harry T
I've missed you so, have you missed me?
You made me feel like a bitch on heat
From the top of my head right down to my feet
Come on over again and fix my fuse
I won't hear 'NO' Harry, so please don't refuse
Harry, Harry, oh Harry T
I want - I need you... to FUCK ME!

The Dog didn't know whether to laugh at the station commander's wife's clumsy attempt at prose, or cry at the helplessness of his situation. The Group Captain was still away in Aden for a few more weeks yet and there was hardly anyone around

70

to notice the odd surreptitious visit to Mrs. Posh Knickers, but Christ! Talk about playing with fire! Needless to say, within two days of Phyllida's visit to the Med Centre, Cpl Thomas had been at her door and letting himself in. In fact, he'd kept on letting himself both into the house and into the very willing Mrs. Parker-Jones, right up until the return of the station commander. Then came the call, the call he'd always knew would come, the big one, the summons to the office of the Station Warrant Officer. He'd been "invited" to an interview as they used to say, without coffee. The hapless NCO had stood tall before the man – the man responsible for dealing with matters of discipline. The SWO had been sitting at his desk, exuding old school military sternness; his grey hair cropped short and gold-rimmed Pince-Nez perched on the end of his aquiline nose. He'd looked up at the offending corporal, standing ramrod straight in front of him and had begun the one-way conversation. It had pretty much gone something to the effect of – he'd been caught poaching; the master of the house had returned to a confession by his wife that she had been shagging a junior rank and he – the SWO had been appointed gamekeeper in the matter.

Upon the return of the conquering hero, his sex mad wife had gleefully informed the unfortunate officer over a glass of sherry, that during his absence, she'd regularly been serviced by one of his men. Oh, and she'd loved it too – the bitch had reveled in the dropping of her little bombshell. After all, when was the last time her husband had been up to the task? She'd taunted the Group Captain with the lurid details of her dirty little secret, humiliated him with it; hadn't given a toss about his feelings and hadn't given a toss about the future of her discarded lover either. The SWO's verdict? Guilty as charged. He'd given Harry forty-eight hours to clear out, pack up and fuck off. The location to which he was to fuck off to? RAF Benbecula - a windswept and distant Hebridean island to the west of Scotland; home to a radar station, a small airbase and little else. Displaying a rare sense of humour, the grizzled old SWO had informed Cpl Thomas that he had better pack some bromide to curb his ardour. There would be nothing remotely feminine in which to "dip his wick" there, he'd said – unless he could get hold of one of the numerous sheep that grazed the heather in the wild interior! With the witticism of the SWO and a barked "NOW GET OUT!" ringing in his ears, the disgraced corporal had trudged unhappily to his

71

quarters and packed up his belongings ready for the long flight north to the land of sheep, crofters and windy hilltop radar sites.

If Harry Thomas had ever nurtured the notion to extend his RAF career, beyond the remaining eighteen months of his contract, the drudgery that was the isle of Benbecula, quickly dispelled such a notion. His contract fulfilled, he boarded the island-hopping Piper Aztec run by the embryonic Logan air and flew away from the sheep, the rain and the Royal Air Force. He'd been given good references despite his indiscretions on Hot Rock and had been well placed to take advantage of the boom in cruise holidays. He'd swapped his RAF wings for sea legs and taken a job as assistant to the ship's surgeon on P&O Orient line's Canberra. On board Canberra, the Dog slowly began to get his old life back; distant exotic shores loomed regularly and there was no shortage of pretty girls giving the handsome medic the eye. He'd indulged, but never knowingly repeated the mistake of poaching another man's wife again – not that such forbidden fruits hadn't been on offer – there was, it seemed, an abundance of sex starved females, all apparently deprived by their husbands! In time, the image of Phyllida Parker-Jones a dim and distant memory, he'd actually come to believe that the old SWO had done him a favour when he'd kicked him out of Malta!

His duties as assistant to the ship's surgeon – himself a retired serviceman – hadn't been dissimilar to his old Med Centre routine of triage. This time though, there hadn't been any cases of blobby knob to deal with; just the odd case of seasickness, sunburn or food poisoning contracted as a result of patients having rashly consumed local food while ashore in some of the less exotic ports of call. Harry the Dog spent ten years cruising the high seas before calling it a day in 1982, not long before the Canberra was requisitioned to act as troopship for the British forces about to retake the Falkland Islands. He'd had the option to stay aboard and look after the civilian crew's medical needs, but cruising into a war zone wasn't his idea of fun, and bidding a reluctant farewell to the old girl, he'd walked down Canberra's gangplank for the last time and into an uncertain future.

The next, or last thirty-five years of Harry's colourful life had whizzed by in a series of odd jobs and it would have been fair to say – odd marriages – three in fact. He'd sired six children and worked in a variety of jobs such as short order cook, estate agent, cable TV installer and postman. He retired at sixty on a mish mash of pensions from the RAF, P&O and the Post Office, which on the face of it, should have kept him quite comfortably; and it would, had it not been for his wives and their claim upon his pension pot. He'd whiled away his retirement in a haze of cigarette smoke and Scotch in some God awful high-rise block in West London, not far from Queens Park Rangers football ground, long since divorced from wife number three. He had rarely ventured out onto the streets now teeming with every race under the sun. The great multicultural experiment foisted upon Britain by the so-called New Labour party, had, in his humble opinion been a giant fuck up. He seldom heard an English voice on the High Street when he nipped out for a newspaper and the only white skins visible were those of Eastern Europeans gulping from their cans of *Tyskie* on darkened street corners before discarding the empties noisily onto the pavement. Going back up to his flat, he'd have to run the gauntlet of feckless, feral youths, their jeans practically falling around their ankles in an imitation of American prison garb. He'd have to dodge pools of spit and piles of dog shit left by the gangster's snarling status dogs.

He'd remembered the words of his father back in the Midlands – every time 'It won't be long now son' In fact, the old lock maker had been saying those words as though death had nigh, for the last ten years of his miserable hump-backed life. Now though, Harry had started to think that the old man had got it right, wishing his life away like that and he'd begun to feel the same. He reflected that his had been a full and interesting life, but he had no desire to prolong it any further. The plans he'd made years before to retire to the sun had long since been thwarted by alimony payments and kids in university, and what with the current financial state of the world, there seemed to be nowhere left to go where his pension would stretch further than in the UK. 'Yes', he'd told the old man staring back at him from the mirror – 'Not long now mate…' And it hadn't been – aged a mere seventy-six years old, Harry the *Dog* had succumbed to lung cancer – a legacy of seventy years of smoking two packs of un-tipped a day. He had known for some time that he'd been ill – he had after all, been given medical training – but he shunned all medical intervention. Not wanting to die bathed in his own piss on some National Health service hospital ward staffed with non-English speaking and apathetic African nurses, he'd died alone and in pain in his shoebox of a flat surrounded by the cacophony of harsh gangsta *rap* echoing around the badly insulated block of flats, domestic arguments, the sound of dogs barking and the incessant wail of police sirens.

CHAPTER NINE
Purgatorial Interactions

'Well at least *you* died of natural causes!'

Harry raised a bushy eyebrow at his old friend's son's comment and countered, 'If you can call cancer a natural cause – and I guess the good lord saw fit to put tobacco into the human equation – then, yes, I suppose it was a kind of natural death!'

'Sorry Harry, I'm talking crap…'

'That's OK young Jake, I guess I've just come to terms with having died. If all was fair back in the world, I wouldn't have been due to meet you again for a few more years yet – assuming that in a few years, I'll still be here!'

Feeling morose, Turner felt devoid of anything suitable to say. The old guy, who'd let him drink his beer back in the day and had turned a dog food diet into a joke, filled the silence as he always had done at parties, during awkward silences and when meeting someone for the first time, by making light of the situation.

'I do get it my old mate' continued Harry, 'And I can understand why you feel cheated. I mean, I had a long and mostly fulfilling life, but towards the end, just like my dad, I found myself wanting it all to be over. I was worn out, in pain and living in a country no longer fit for heroes. You, on the other hand, were probably robbed of about thirty years and numerous bloody good shags!'

There it was again; the old Harry humour and he was glad of it, glad to be in this place with someone he'd once felt close to. It lifted him and took the edge of his sadness.

'From what you've told me old timer, I've had a lucky escape – losing out in the shag department – I mean, you didn't exactly cover yourself in glory back in *your* shagging days!'

'Very funny! I enjoyed every minute – well almost – apart from the SWO tearing me a new asshole when I got caught out with Mrs. Posh Knickers*!'*

'Seriously though Harry, what are we doing here? How long are we to be in suspended animation do you think? It's like waiting for a bus that never comes! And what about those people I can see but never reach? What about my army buddy Len? If he's been dead for as long as I think he has – and believe me, I'm starting to doubt my grip on time – then what are the chances of us getting out of here anytime soon, if ever?'

It was the Dog's turn to be reflective. 'I don't know mate, I really haven't a clue; I guess we're just going to have to adjust. I mean, it's not as if it's a bad place to be; we're not hungry, cold or in pain…'

'We *just are…*' they said simultaneously before falling silent again, each wrapped in some distant worldly memory.

After another *Pethidine* pause, Jake opened his eyes to find Harry gone and Sarah Tunney looking down at him. Her quiet presence was a welcome distraction from his dark Purgatorial musings and smiling up at her, he beckoned for her to sit down next to him.

'Hi Sarah, I was beginning to wonder where you'd got to'

Smiling sadly, she sat down. 'I don't know where I've been Jake, I really don't. Time – if you can call it that – just fades away. I seem to spend most of my time in some kind of trance and when I'm not, I just find myself wandering around this endless place. I see people – at least I think they're people, but I never seem to get any closer to them; they just evaporate like fog in the sun'

The girl looked and sounded desperate. 'I'm so fuckin' lonely Jake that if I wasn't dead, I'd wish I was!'

The dead cop and his hooker friend laughed; despite their predicament, they giggled like children. The laughter was short-lived and was born more out of hysteria than mirth. After the laughter had subsided, Turner couldn't really think of anything more to say, managing only a, 'Yeah, know what you mean love…'

'It's hard to explain really' Sarah rejoined; 'I'm neither happy nor sad; I'm not hungry or thirsty; most of all though, I don't have any other needs. I don't want booze, I don't want to smoke and as for crack pipes, fuck that shit!'

Turner nodded empathetically, smiling inwardly at the girl's coarse turn of phrase. "You can take the girl out of the gutter" he thought, but "you can't take the gutter out of the girl!"

He liked her though; liked her grit; with a heartfelt sigh he wearily rubbed at his face, before peering out at Sarah through his fingers. Smiling he joked: 'Shame we had to die to sort our shit out though eh?'

He immediately regretted his choice of words when the poor girl began sobbing. Pulling her close, he stroked the distraught girl's hair, whispering in her ear in an attempt to undo the damage.

76

'Sssh... Sarah, don't cry love, you were in a world of shit back there with no way out. You're safe here, nobody can harm you – no more drugs, no more disgusting men sweating over you and no crack consuming your soul'

She looked up at him, her face streaked with tears, 'I was in a world of shit, but at least I was alive. Not much of a life I know – but here? What the fuck is *here*? Have I got a soul? Am I a soul? Is this all there is? I wanna' go home Jake, I'm scared!'

He hadn't admitted it before, the hard bitten ex-soldier, the cynical cop – but holding the junkie girl close, feeling the sobs wracking her body – he felt scared too – shit scared of the future; if there was to be such a thing in this place. He hadn't been immune to all that biblical bullshit, spoon-fed to him since Sunday school. What if there was a heaven and a hell? He knew for a fact that he hadn't been good enough to merit going to heaven and as for confession; it was many a long year since he'd said Hail Mary's to absolve him of the sins made up for the benefit of the priest behind the curtain. Hell? Was it really some Dante Inferno with forked tailed demons in attendance? Was it really somewhere where drinks refused to come out of bottles? While on the subject of demons - Jake time flashed...

Back in the world as a rookie cop, PC Turner had been dispatched to what he thought was yet another routine domestic disturbance. The call to his radio had been received right at the end of a long and uneventful night shift - when tired and lethargic - he'd only really registered the words argument, mother and daughter. These words, crackling over his radio usually constituted a domestic argument; the like of which seemed to account for sixty percent of police work. Domestics didn't tend to generate much enthusiasm – not really surprising when domestic calls actually included such crap as a female calling the emergency number to report that her boyfriend had taken the TV remote control and was refusing to give it back! His senses dulled by the long and uneventful night shift, he'd not really caught the full gist of what the call had been about, and climbing wearily into his patrol car he'd made his way to the scene of the domestic. Upon arrival, he found that he had been beaten to it by a sergeant, who'd clearly been more switched on as to what had really happened at the drab house on the council estate.

Jake had got there a few minutes after the sergeant, who with another constable, was trying to gain entry to the house. The front door was open, but something that felt spongy yet unyielding, was preventing the door opening fully. Jake lent a hand and between the three of them, they managed to push the door open just enough to squeeze through the gap one at a time. Once inside, they soon discovered the nature of the spongy obstruction – it was none other than the still warm body of the woman who just minutes earlier had generated the call to PC Turner's radio. She'd ended up wedged between the bottom step of the steep staircase and the front door. The hilt of a large Bowie knife was just visible, buried between the woman's narrow shoulders. She'd been stabbed with such force, that a post mortem would later find the tip of the hunting knife had lodged in her sternum.

Going upstairs, and into a bedroom, the officers had found another body, that of an elderly man. He'd also been stabbed and had collapsed onto the bed, his life force staining the floral quilt with crimson pools and tingeing the air with that ferrous smell of fresh blood. Jake, by now racked with the guilt of his initial cynical and slow reaction to the call, waited downstairs, sharing the tiny hallway with the crumpled corpse of the domestic, the woman who must have died during the call she'd made to the police. The desperate call for help – no argument over a remote control this time – but the frantic pleas of a mother begging the police to come and stop her daughter killing her husband. It appeared to Jake that mum had been at the top of the stairs calling 999 from the remote phone, when having killed her father, the girl plunged Mr. Bowie's lethal creation between mum's shoulder blades killing her instantly and causing her to tumble down the stairs. The unfortunate woman had come to rest up against the front door where her bloodied nightie-clad body, had performed the impromptu and macabre duties of a draught excluder.

The sergeant appeared at the top of the stairs accompanied by the other officer and a young woman, who, save for a flimsy pair of g-string panties was completely naked. She was dyed head to toe in the unmistakable muddy brown colour of arterial blood, already flakily drying in the centrally heated house and giving her the appearance of some Papuan warrior daubed in rich rain forest mud – not unlike those 1960's images of the flower power festival revelers at Woodstock. "No peace and love in this house - the same drugs maybe" Jake thought grimly – just a girl driven insane by years of drug taking. A girl, who in her psychosis and neglected by the system, had become convinced that her elderly parents, had been the devil incarnate. The voices in her head had, utterly convinced her that mum and dad were demons and that they must die. The cruel voices had become intolerably strident early that fateful morning, remorselessly propelling the drug crazed girl into her parent's bedroom, where she'd wordlessly attacked her father with the Bowie knife, kept out of paranoia under her pillow. Her mother had got as far as the upstairs landing where she'd made the frantic call to the police, before she too had been dispatched with the ruthless efficiency of her offspring, bent as she had been, on exorcising the demons that had taken over her drug addicted life.

As she'd been led, firmly but not without sympathy, out of the front door, her g-string had caught on the door latch, tearing the flimsy material and causing the tattered remnants to hang pathetically by a thread, exposing a white triangle, stark against the dried blood of her parents which covered her naked body. Police Constable Jake Turner had learned a valuable lesson that morning, and would never again anticipate the nature of a call – domestic or otherwise. The post-incident *wash-up*, carried out by the duty inspector in the company of all those involved – emergency call takers and officers - would absolve them all of blame. It was apparent, that when the distraught woman had initially called to report her husband being attacked, he was already dead. As for her, she'd been dead the minute she had made the call – callously and savagely stabbed, she would have been dead before her body hit the last step in the house where her little girl had been born and grew up.

Coming back to, like some victim of narcolepsy, Jake thought grimly - not for the first time since he'd arrived in that place - that he seemed destined to dwell on his many mistakes made back in the world. *Surely,* he mused, he must have done *something* right – or was this the "life flashing before your eyes" phenomenon often talked about by mere mortals? No, it couldn't be – he'd always thought that was something that only applied to near death experiences – and he was beyond *near* death – wasn't he? Turner looked around – Sarah had once again disappeared during his latest

79

reverie. "Typical" he thought disconsolately – "Just like falling asleep on the couch next to the missus halfway through some chick flick or other"

'Some things never change' he muttered, then found himself involuntarily reciting the only bit of a prayer he could remember:

'On earth as it is in heaven…'

Somewhere in the vast depths of the place a sinewy, aggressive looking young man was staring angrily into space, his eyes spitting icy spears of pure hatred at anyone who had the misfortune to look his way. Dressed in jeans that were halfway down his bony ass, he wore glitzy unlaced training shoes and a Hollister hoodie; he oozed street scum. His name - this ball of venom – back in the world - had been Michael Casey. He'd been a wrong 'un, a criminal and in the vernacular of cops such as Jake Turner – he'd been a shit – a scrote – a fuckin' scumbag and an oxygen thief. Being in this place, this world of the dead, hadn't done much to cause him to mellow either. The only thing that caused his cruel mouth to contort into the resemblance of a smile had been the girl, who having walked past him, came to an abrupt halt, before walking back into his view.

Leaving Turner to another of his Pethidine reveries, Sarah Tunney left the cop's side and strolled aimlessly along the seemingly endless expanse of bland white concourse. She hadn't got very far, before she saw the "bastard" an unwelcome interloper to her new present from her miserable past. Large as life and twice as ugly, the bastard reclined right there in front of her; all sneering bravado, sovereign rings, and a tacky heavy-duty necklace from which swung a pair of boxing gloves. Sarah remembered that particular piece of jewellery well. She'd witnessed him beat half to death the former owner of it during a botched robbery. The poor bastard may have worn the miniature boxing gloves around his neck, and they may have signified membership of some boxing gym or other, but staggering home under the influence of too many cheap lagers, he hadn't been a match for the bastard and his knuckleduster adorned fists.

The bastard called her over. Sneering, he spoke as if he were a Jamaican gangster, a "yardie" – not that he had ever been any further than a day trip to Calais, let alone Trench Town. His voice heavy with the scorn of a victor used to speaking to the vanquished, he scoffed, 'Wagwaan? Wha' you doin' ere bitch?'

She remembered both the fear and affection she used to have for the bastard; all gone now, sluiced away like yesterday's washing up water – washed away and swirling down the greasy plughole. Here, in *this place,* she no longer felt fear nor the earthly chains of her former life. Fuck him, and fuck all the other tossers who back in the world had ruled her drug-dependent life. Tunney looked the bastard right in the eye.

'Go fuck yourself you skinny piece of shit!'

The bastard wasn't happy, wasn't used to being spoken to like that; especially by some junkie bitch he'd had a hold over back in the world. Who the fuck did this stinking whore think she was talking to? Hatred and volcanic anger welled up inside him, but try as he might; he just wasn't able to do anything about it. He felt totally immobile, like the first time he'd smoked skunk – the mind was willing but the body refused to respond. He felt as though an unseen hand was pressing down on his head, preventing him from getting up and slapping the bitch. Sarah, totally unafraid, looked down at him and laughed - no humour - just a hollow laugh that said, "Fuck you!"

Leaving the bastard, his mouth opening and closing, thin cruel lips flecked with spittle, she turned on her heel and walked away, her chest swelling with the unfamiliar pride of victory. "I may be dead" she thought, and then aloud: 'But here, in this place, I've got my life back' Then, smiling at her own reference to life, in what was obviously death, she continued her aimless strolling – looking, if truth be known - for the only person who'd ever showed her compassion – the cop, the dead cop, brought to her by means of the Victoria line tube train to Brixton…

CHAPTER TEN
Michael's Story

On the day that Michael Casey slithered out from between his mother's legs, and on to the delivery table, his father Mickey, had been three months into a fourteen-year stretch at Wormwood Scrubs for armed robbery. A career criminal, it hadn't been his first bout of incarceration at Her Majesty's Pleasure and on that occasion, Casey senior had been ensnared by the DNA left in his balaclava, carelessly discarded not far from the scene of what had been his latest criminal endeavour. It wasn't that he was normally that careless; but due to a snitch in the pay of a source handler of the Metropolitan police, he'd panicked and been obliged to dump the incriminating piece of evidence in a wheelie bin at the end of the rubbish strewn alleyway, through which he'd made his unplanned escape.

The filth had been all over the post office job not long after it's inception; he and the rest of the gang had been under surveillance night and day for the two week run up to the job. It wasn't often that the old bill got such a break; the majority of so called tip offs usually came to nothing. The junkie informant had earned his money on this one though; he'd been close to Casey and even closer to his wife. Taking the chance to get him out of the way for a while and to claim a few quid for the information, he'd ensured that the entire gang of four was behind bars and on remand within a week of the bungled robbery. The surveillance boys hadn't been the usual locals – blatantly obvious in their black *Berghaus* fleece jackets, *Merrell* cross trainers and shaven heads, nor had they been driving around in the unmarked Ford Mondeo's known to even the most obtuse of petty criminals in the area. They hadn't been caught out by the sudden and unexpected loud bursts from their police radios and they hadn't been the blatant white skinned exception in a London borough where the only white skins were that of eastern Europeans. These guys were the real deal, professionals used to tracking terror suspects for weeks on end, men and women who wouldn't merit a second glance on the run down council estates on which they plied their trade. The men and women of the Specialist Crime Directorate

(11) were the real deal and they'd done for Casey's gang in a big way.

SCD (11) had spent the fortnight watching the Casey home from an observation point in the front bedroom of a retired hospital matron, who'd been glad of the company and glad of the opportunity to busy herself making cups of tea and chunky sandwiches for her resident watchers. She'd happily decamped to the spare room at the back of her house for the duration, and pretty much left them to it. Primarily, this OP had been set up to observe and document the Casey's comings and goings and was known in surveillance jargon as "establishing lifestyle." Awash with strong tea, their stomachs crying out for relief from the constant supply of well meant sandwiches, the cops had amused themselves, observing the comings and goings of the Casey household. Old man Casey's every move was reported back to the control room and his movements passed on to the mobile units in place to take up the follow, when he left the house. His missus was also of interest to the watchers, and it hadn't been too long before the main motivation driving the snitch had become clear. They'd followed the wife off as she had driven away from the house in her custard yellow VW Beetle – the new model - restyled on the original classic favourite, complete with it's obligatory gerbera daisy in the dashboard vase. They'd followed Mrs. Casey to the rural rendezvous with her husband's betrayer and watched the woman's legs – magnified by their powerful lenses – as she swung them onto the dashboard, next to the gerbera. With most of his body unseen by the followers, they could just make out the top of the informant's head, from where he crouched in the Beetle's passenger side foot well, his face buried in Mrs. Casey's crotch. The custard yellow Beetle, had not only been in sight electronically and physically, but the detectives monitoring the audio back at the station, had also been treated to the adulterous moans and groans of Mrs. Casey as their informant carried out his tongue gymnastics in the confines of the Beetle's foot well. His performance had elicited such coarse offerings as: 'Get in there my son!' and 'Way down south where the tuna fish play'

On two occasions, 11 had followed Casey senior off from his house, where he'd met up with the other post office conspirators and carried out reconnaissance, of several possible targets around the northwest area of London. The gang was already suspected of having carried out at least three other post office robberies across the capital, but it hadn't been until Casey's wife's lover had broken cover, that they'd been able to apply for RIPA authority to watch him. The Regulation of Investigatory Powers Act of 2000, had cut down drastically on the previous numbers of ad hoc surveillance jobs undertaken by the police, customs, the armed forces and other governmental organisations. The act had put in place various safeguards – often influenced by case law - to prevent abuse of the system. Intrusive surveillance authority, which the detectives managed to secure in the case of the post office job, was as good as it got for the followers. It could be argued, that a little gilding of the lily had been exercised by the detectives, when seeking permission for intrusive surveillance; but once this authority was in place, they'd had *carte blanche* to bug Casey's house, vehicles and his work place. Intrusive surveillance was top of the tree when it came to RIPA, with the act stipulating that it could be employed in the interests of national security, for the purpose of preventing or detecting serious crime and in the interests of the economic well being of the United Kingdom.

As well as wiring Casey's car and that of his wife for sound, the 11 boys had lumped both the cars for good measure. The *lump* was slang for the device, which would track Casey's car and give the watchers the option of following it electronically in areas difficult for the surveillance teams to get into. As good as they were, there were some places where they'd stick out like sore thumbs. The drinkers in some of the council estate pubs that Casey frequented could spot a stranger a mile off and such close up work was more suited to the brave officers who carried out the work of undercover men and women. These cops would be well and truly embedded in the community with established cover stories that stretched back, in some cases, for years. The team working Casey, however, had been assembled at short notice and hadn't had the luxury of inserting the UC people. SCD had also deployed a backup observation point in the form of a "carpet van" This had been parked across from the Greyhound public House. A regular haunt of the Casey gang, the Greyhound was situated on a main road, which split in two a rundown 1950's council estate, known locally as the "poets" - it's streets misleadingly named as they were, after famous writers of romantic poems. The pub's catchment area mainly consisted of the welfare dependent all day drinkers from the estate, and it had been doubtful whether any of the residents could have recited any of Keats' classics. The carpet van, to the casual dog walker appeared to be just that – the rear windows were filled with carpet rolls – the tubes of which afforded a decent rear view and the sides of the van were fitted with pin-hole cameras, affording views left and right. A front facing camera completed the all round vision with a heavy book of carpet samples adorning the dashboard along with copies of tabloid newspapers, drinks cans and empty sandwich wrappers. An identical book of samples would be taken from the van by the driver, once it had been put into place, and exiting the vehicle, he'd be seen by anyone who cared, ostensibly trudging off around the estate, samples in hand, going about his round of cold calling. The operatives inside would be left for the day and sometimes night, with a thermos of coffee and whatever food they'd taken with them for the vigil ahead. As for toiletry needs, the boys and girls of SCD (11) had long since learned not to be bashful when pissing in full view of their colleagues, into the issued receptacles stowed underneath the seats of the cramped van.

On the day of the robbery, 11 had followed the gang off from their meeting point under the railway arches off the Kilburn Highroad. They'd got into a white, nondescript Ford Transit van – on false plates and recently stolen from a van hire company – before driving off in the direction of the notorious South Kilburn Estate. The estate was just inside Brent Borough, on the fringes of fashionable Notting Hill in the Royal Borough of Kensington and Chelsea. It may have been located next to the fashionable borough which was home to such tourist traps as Harrods and the Albert Hall, but, geography was the only thing the shit hole shared with it's millionaire neighbours. The stolen van presented a problem for the surveillance teams, as without a tracking device, it would be game over for the follow should it be lost in traffic. Once inside the labyrinth that was home to some of the most dangerous gangs in North West London, they'd picked up another stolen vehicle also bearing false plates – this time a powerful Audi Quattro A4, into which two of their number got into. Driving in convoy, they headed off down the Kilburn High Road, choked as always with buses and frustrated drivers, who'd been foolish enough to try and negotiate

85

what was a hopelessly outdated thoroughfare and no better than a third world mess of honking vehicles all trying to make the torturous journey west, either to the M1 motorway, the M4 or the A40 towards Oxford.

It had taken all the skills that the surveillance people had possessed to follow both the Transit van and the Audi. As good as the snitch's information had been, it hadn't stretched to the location of the robbery, just the day on which it had been planned to take place. The one thing in their favour, had been the route selected by the would- be robbers. The cops tailing the vehicles had experienced no trouble at all in staying close to the small convoy in the bumper-to-bumper rat race that was the Kilburn High Road. In fact, these conditions had persisted all the way through to Cricklewood Broadway and it hadn't become tricky until the bad guy's vehicles had reached the nightmare of a road junction that was the Hanger Lane gyratory system. The word gyratory may have conjured up visions of a smooth traffic system at which drivers courteously and seamlessly interacted, but the reality of Hanger Lane was that of a multi lane – multi directional maelstrom of motorists, sick and tired of long delays, impatiently jockeying for last minute positions in the confused atmosphere of the place.

In the event, the followers of team one had managed to follow the gang's convoy west and onto the A40 towards Oxford, where, at the Perivale junction, the cops had had their first piece of luck. Turning off, the gang's van took the next left into the petrol station, where the occupants got out; one to fill the tank with diesel, with the other disappearing into the station's shop. The Audi hadn't followed the Transit onto the garage forecourt, but having turned off at the same time, it stopped in a lay-by just beyond. This had been the surveillance team's second stroke of luck and the minute the driver of the Transit had gone into the kiosk to pay for his fuel, one of the 11 girls, posing as a motorist checking her engine oil, whipped up the bonnet of their car and cast an eye over to the kiosk. There were at least three people in the queue to pay before the Transit's driver's turn came, and providing somebody didn't ring the till bell to summon another cashier to deal with the line of customers before she could make her move – providing the van's passenger didn't return early from his shit in the stinking toilets – she just may have had enough time… Making a snap decision which was the necessary hallmark of her profession, the girl had casually, but quickly walked over to the paper towel dispenser, where after pulling a few of the coarse green towels out, she'd expertly dropped a set of keys onto the greasy forecourt next to the Transit. Bending down, she'd lumped the underside of the gang's van and strolled calmly back to her waiting colleagues. She rejoined them to an admiring chorus of: "That was fuckin' close!"

It looked as though, the gang's recces of the original London locations, had either been deemed to risky or else they'd got wind of the surveillance operation against them. Either way, if whatever their planned target had been was still in play, they were sure as hell taking a circuitous route to get there. The watchers expressed reluctant admiration of the balls the gang was displaying in traveling such long distances in the stolen vehicles. All it would have taken was the keen eye of a traffic cop to stop them in their tracks. A keen scrutiny of the windscreen Vehicle Identification Number would have been all that it took to note that it didn't tally with the stolen number plates. One look at the VIN would have scuppered both the plans of the robbers and the pursuing SCD teams.

Once all of the players had returned to their vehicles, team one had followed the Transit out onto the slip road, where it had picked up the waiting Audi and rejoined the A40. It had come as a relief when they'd been able to hand the tail over to a fresh set of wheels, giving them time to try and anticipate the gang's route and leapfrog to the next handover point. Picking up the convoy, the new team had followed the Transit and the Audi along the A40, which after a while became the M40. They stayed with the robbery suspects as far as the turn off for the A41, where fearing compromise, and lacking fast time support so far north, they'd reluctantly entrusted the next leg of the journey to the data fed back by the risky ad hoc lump placed by the girl from 11.

Team one, who'd handed over eyeball of the convoy on the A40, had been kept informed with regard to their quarry's progress and likely destination; then as planned, had leapfrogged their colleagues in a high speed scramble getting ahead of both the hunters and the hunted and resuming the follow. The girl's lump had indicated that the bandit vehicles were somewhere south of Aylesbury and still on the A41 heading north. Aylesbury was a potential loss point, surrounded as it was by innumerable roundabouts, one-way systems and possible destinations. Realising the importance of not depending wholly on electronics and the haphazard signals the lump gave off in rural areas, team one had busted a gut to pick the convoy up before they reached their destination. There seemed no doubt that this was more than just a run through and spirits was running high among the cops. Meanwhile, teams of armed officers, from the Metropolitan police and by now armed response vehicles of their Thames Valley colleagues, were well and truly in the loop of what was shaping up to be a good day's work.

Thanks to the lump and the timely coincidence of a slow moving tractor, the original team had been able to pick up the gang's convoy as it became stuck behind the lumbering agricultural machine in the tiny village of Rowsham. A hasty appraisal of the map showed the followers that the only post office between Rowsham and the Bedfordshire town of Leighton Buzzard was to be found on the high street of Wing, three miles further along the A418. Following the crooks along this rural stretch had been tricky, particularly once they'd overtaken the tractor, but with very few turnoffs of note before Wing – and the A418 being the main route north – team one managed to keep the tail without arousing suspicion. Entering the picturesque outskirts of Wing, excitement began to mount among the SCD operatives – could Wing be the target? Surely Leighton Buzzard would be too much of a challenge – too big a town for the gang to risk making move? It wasn't as if they were on the threshold of a good arterial route upon which to make their escape and what with the availability of not only Bedfordshire's police air support helicopter, but also that of Thames Valley, they'd be sitting ducks in this open country. One of the wags in team one's car, had remarked with more than a little irony, that this was Great Train Robbery country. Not too many miles from where they were, was Hawkslade farm – the disastrous hideout of Ronnie Biggs and his gang back in the 60's. Could this be a nod of respect towards those villains of yesteryear?

Ajit Devar had run the village sub post office inn Wing for the last twenty-five years. Treated with suspicion when he'd first taken over the post office from the about to retire Hilda and Jim Brown, he'd gradually earned the respect of the locals, who'd admired his work ethic. Open all hours, he'd transformed the little shop from somewhere that sold irrelevant odds and ends to a mini-supermarket, in which although the prices were a little high, the older members of the village community, had welcomed the fact that they no longer had to take the infrequent bus service into Leighton Buzzard to pick up their groceries.

Ajit had been just about to close up for the afternoon when all hell broke loose. His front door crashed open, sending the little genteel bell that hung above it careering noisily into the air and embedding itself into the illuminated sign, which advertised the latest addition to his repertoire – *Krispy Kreme* donuts. Crashing into Ajit's orderly world came Casey and his three balaclava clad heavies. Casey had led the assault, and leaping over the counter, he'd thrust a sawn-off shotgun into the face of the postmaster, snarling, that the "Fuckin' Indian monkey was to hand over the cash from the till and the contents of the back room safe" Of the other three hoodlums, two remained by the front door pickaxe handles at the ready while the third sprinted to the back of the shop to secure the back door. Recovering from his initial shock Ajit – whose Hindi name meant "Invincible" riled at the insult of "Indian monkey" Had not his father gallantly served the British army during World War Two? Hadn't he worked every hour that the God Brahman had been gracious enough to send him? Was he going to allow this white trash to take away his honour? It hadn't been so much a thought process – more like a temporary wave of unadulterated rage that gave him the inexplicable strength of a mother lifting a car off her children after an accident. In this case, the mother was Ajit, the children, his shop and insanity reigned.

Without a care for his mortal body, the hitherto mild mannered Devar saw red for the first time in his hard working life. Ignoring the very real danger of the sawn off, it's barrels gaping like twin train tunnels in front of his face, he made his move. Dropping swiftly to his knees within the confines of his cluttered shop counter, he grabbed hold of the bewildered gang boss's ankles, at the same time, cannoning his balding head into Casey's groin. Pulling with a strength he hadn't known he'd possessed, the Invincible One – son of the war hero – toppled the would be robber, and sent him crashing against the lottery machine with such force that he lost the grip on his shotgun, which clattered harmlessly to the floor. The momentum of the Indian's attack, cracked Casey's head against the edge of the well-worn counter like a bullwhip. His brain set alight by a thousand blinding stars of pain, it had been all he could do to remain conscious. Staggering towards the rear of Ajit's empire, the fight gone out of him, he'd managed to locate the fire doors, and leaving his gang to make their own escape arrangements, he'd fled down an alleyway that led onto the only council estate in the area, ditching his balaclava in the first wheelie bin he could find.

Right at this point in proceedings, another group of men had burst through the doors of sub postmaster Devar. This time though, they'd been in the form of the Met's CO19 bristling with the tools of their trade - MP5's, Glock handguns and ballistic helmets which wouldn't have looked out of place in Star Wars. With repeated yelled commands of "POLICE! GET ON THE FLOOR!" they'd crashed into and through the little shop and rounded up Casey's by now leaderless gang, who they'd found cowering inside a tiny outside storeroom on the hard standing at the rear of the post office. Face down and prone in the dirt, all bravado gone their hands bound by the oversized cable ties known as plasticuffs, the hapless trio didn't need a fortuneteller to predict their future. At least one of them though, would need a change of underwear, soaked as it was by the contents of a bladder involuntarily emptying. The short circuit between brain and urethral sphincter, had come in the very instant it's owner had been confronted by the savagery of 19's extreme, but controlled violence. Speed aggression and surprise - this was the hallmark of SO19, and it hadn't been the first time that grown men had pissed themselves in their presence.

Just Before the mayhem of SO19 had been unleashed; team one had observed the Transit pull off Wing High Street and into the car park of the sports field opposite the post office, closely followed by the Quattro. They had wondered – the professional watchers – why the entire gang had got out of the vehicles to commit the robbery. Why – they had mused – hadn't at least one person been left behind to drive the getaway vehicle? They'd either been too short on the ground (keep the numbers down to avoid leaks) or cocky enough to stroll away after the robbery and do one in the Audi. Their part in the operation complete, they'd observed from their rural grandstand viewpoint, the professional aggression, unleashed by the firearms boys as they visited shock and awe upon the unsuspecting villains. Immersed in their self-congratulatory backslapping, they'd failed to notice old man Casey as he'd slipped snake-like, away from the scene. Licking his wounds, the gangster - out of his comfort zone in the rural setting gone wrong - had staggered from the rear of the post office, trying desperately to fight off the nauseous effects of the unexpected attack wreaked upon him by the mild mannered Hindu postmaster.

Casting an experienced eye over the cars parked either side of the estate; Casey's blurred vision had alighted upon an old Ford Fiesta parked at the end of a cul-de-sac. Within seconds, he'd forced the door lock with a screwdriver, pulled out the antiquated ignition wires and employing the methods learned as a teenager from the older boys joyriding stolen cars around his estate, he'd quickly identified the relevant wires. Touching the sparking wires together, and footing the accelerator pedal, he'd eventually coaxed the spluttering engine into life. Assuming that the police net would quickly tighten, he'd got the hell off the estate and driven the little red car along the back roads until he reached the M1 motorway, which would return him to the sanctity of north London, where he could call in favours and disappear until the dust settled. In his wildest dreams, Casey hadn't reckoned on the fury of the little Indian guy at the Wing post office. He also hadn't reckoned on the skill and patience of the follow up search team, who'd quickly found the balaclava, discarded in an unguarded moment – the moment when, still reeling from his sudden and unexpected contact with the post office counter, and the ferocity of the curry eating bastard – his head full of shooting stars of pain - he'd succumbed to the careless urge to ditch his disguise. It had been his undoing, that careless mistake and the weedy bespectacled Thames Valley Scenes Of Crime Officer had triumphantly exhibited the incriminating item, before bagging it up in a brown paper exhibits bag and sending it off to the forensics lab. It had provided a wealth of evidence, that woolly piece of headgear – saliva from around the mouth area and hair from the gangster's head – all evidential gold in the form of the villain's DNA.

Casey had been careful enough not to come to the attention of the police since the legislation, in May 2004 - which under the Police and Criminal Evidence Act, ruled that all those arrested for a recordable offence would have to give a sample of their DNA. Taken as a buccal swab from inside the cheek, the sample could be taken by force if necessary. Michael's father had fallen foul of the "positive arrest policy" for matters of domestic violence, and after giving Mrs. Casey a slap late one night for staying out late, he'd ended up being nicked by the Old Bill, after his daughter had panicked and called 999. It wasn't as if the hard pressed officers of the Metropolitan police gave a toss about scumbags knocking their wives around; but well publicised cases of domestic abuse had ended in the odd murder and hadn't looked good for the figures. As a result, all allegations of domestic disharmony – be it between brothers, sisters, mothers, fathers, lovers – gay or otherwise – had to be resolved by arresting the offender – just in case…

And so it had come to pass, that old man Casey had found himself nicked and processed for common assault on his wife and as part of the process, he'd inadvertently joined the ranks of those whose criminals – petty or otherwise – who's DNA languished in the police freezer awaiting the day when it could be matched to the scene of a crime. This, was how he'd been caught for his part in the bungled robbery and the reason he'd been absent for the birth of his second child – Michael Casey…

Old man Casey had played the game in the Scrubs, and a result, taken advantage of the ridiculous British justice system which allowed for the release of a prisoner at the halfway point of his already lenient sentence, should he show himself to be a model prisoner. Six and a half years later, and out on parole, he'd been greeted by his long-suffering wife and the six-year old son, he'd last just about acknowledged as a bump.

Growing up with his father's indoctrination that all cops were bastards, hadn't been the best start to young Michael's life and after the first six years of being a fairly normal kid who'd respected the authority of school; upon the reappearance of old man Casey, he'd slowly but surely, began to go off the rails. His Dad's reputation spared him any schoolyard bullying, and it hadn't been long before he had started pushing the boundaries set by the adults around him. Aged eleven, he'd begun to skip school, instead, choosing to hang around the shopping malls with other like-minded kids, and his own criminal career had been launched on the day he'd successfully evaded detection, having stolen a DVD from record store. It wasn't as though he'd *wanted* the DVD – he'd long since outgrown computer generated cartoon films – it had been more a case of needing to experience the thrill of getting away with doing it. Before too long, bored with stealing insignificant items, Casey junior had teamed up with a couple of other boys and taken to snatching money from unwary users of ATMs. They'd kept this up until the day they'd fallen foul of a gang of "Lebanese loopers" (despite the name, these devices weren't used by criminals from Lebanon, but were mainly employed by eastern Europeans) These people were nasty and meant business – they'd gone to a lot of trouble and expense to manufacture and place the devices onto ATMs and until the practice became widespread, the public at large had made easy pickings. The devices were made to look like a natural addition to the front of the cash dispenser, but once a card was inserted into the slot as normal, it would be retained by the device - it's PIN having been detected. Assuming the machine was faulty and had "swallowed" their card, the hapless victims would wander off leaving it captured in the crooks contraption. Sometimes cameras would be incorporated to record PIN details, or else, a crude piece of plastic would be placed over the slot to retain the card. This was a much cheaper option and would involve one of the gang standing in the queue behind the user, acting as a friendly adviser while looking over a shoulder to see the PIN. Whatever the method, the scammers were always nearby in order to retrieve lost cards, but more importantly, their devices. They weren't averse to using violence to retain the loops and had been even known to fight with police officers called out to investigate dodgy ATMs.

Standing around an isolated cash machine one morning waiting for a victim, Casey junior had been approached by a swarthy looking Romanian with a livid pink scar running from eye to chin. His wild eyes had terrified even the petty thief and he'd instantly known that scar face wasn't to be fucked with. He'd worked this out seconds before the Romanian had whipped out the nasty looking switchblade knife and spreading his hands in a gesture of defeat, he'd skulked away taking his equally frightened mates with him. Of course, this hadn't meant the end of Casey's fledgling criminal career, just a change to the way that he made money, and seeing the ease with which drug dealers pocketed cash, he'd earned the trust of an Afghan dealer and become one of his many runners.

London – along with the rest of the country had become awash with cannabis; in fact, so much of it was grown in nondescript suburban houses, that Britain had actually become an exporter of the stuff. Predominantly Vietnamese immigrants would pay a year's rent in advance in hard cash, to greedy Asian landlords who asked no questions. The houses would be gutted and turned into cannabis factories producing thousands of pounds worth of "*skunk*" each week. The "gardeners" were generally fellow Vietnamese, smuggled into the country on the backs of trucks via Calais. Kept as virtual prisoners without identity documents, they tended to their bosses stinking but profitable crops, living and sleeping in the only tiny space of the houses not turned over to cultivation. Every now and then, acting on a tip off from a suspicious neighbour (funny smells, windows covered over in tin foil and the odd sighting of an oriental) the police would execute a drugs warrant at the addresses, having first employed the air support unit to overfly the property. Fitted with infrared cameras, the helicopter observer would easily detect any abnormal heat source generated by the hydroponics setup, emanating from the roof. This amount of heat was generally a good indication that the cultivation of cannabis was taking place a few hundred feet below their aerial platform. Normally, by the time the police came crashing through the front door, the gardeners had long since become suspicious, having noticed some over zealous local cop carrying out a pre-warrant recce, but every now and then someone would be caught inside. They'd be arrested, interviewed first by the cops and then by officers from the border agency. Once it had become obvious that the illegal immigrants had disposed of their identity documents upon entry through the porous UK borders, the immigration officials would simply make the suspects promise to turn up at the local immigration centre for processing. Not believing their luck – or possibly knowing full well that this was the drill, they'd of course, agree to this before disappearing into the overcrowded streets of London never to be seen again.

Despite increased CCTV coverage and extra cops on patrol, the runners had been practically able to ply their trade with impunity. If they were nabbed, they were careful never to be caught with more than a couple of £20 bags and even then, lazy cops tended to employ the latest figure massaging option of issuing a street warning. It hadn't been surprising that Casey had taken to his latest criminal activities with the confidence of having little, if any judicial consequence. Before long, he'd moved up the chain and begun to sell the odd bag for himself. This hadn't always gone smoothly though, and he'd had to watch his back and make sure he didn't stray onto other dealers' territory. Knives and even guns were a common and sure-fire way of dealing with competition, and Casey junior had learned the rules fast. Not all the cops in his town had been lazy though and informants – either in need of cash or out of rivalry – had ensured that his house had been raided several times in the search for drugs and cash to seize under the new Proceeds of Crime Act. POCA was the scourge of criminals further up the food chain and empowered officers to seize not only unaccounted for cash, but also assets such as TVs, cars and jewellery. Any items seized under POCA had to be claimed back through the courts, and unlike criminal offences; the owners were not entitled to free legal representation. Many crumbled and acquiesced, either not attending court at all or being totally unable to account for their riches. Police canteens the length and breadth of the capital had benefitted from the unclaimed confiscations in the form of huge flat screen TVs claimed from the dealers.

Casey junior had soon become a substantial blip on the police radar and although the evidence had consisted of little more than third hand information, they'd been exhorted by their senior officers to keep the Casey's on their toes and in so doing, tick the boxes on the reports submitted to the weekly meetings with the top brass. The Casey family had grown used to the dawn raids and long since tired of replacing their front door, smashed open as it usually was, under the impact of the thirty-five pounds of red metal known officially as the *enforcer* or more colloquially, the "big red key" Depending on the skill of the officer wielding the enforcer, it usually took between one and six hits to break down the door. Wooden ones were easy, but UPVC doors offered more resistance due to their flexibility. No matter the amount of hits, the forced entry was normally followed by up to ten hairy-assed cops in riot helmets bursting into the house and exerting total control over the occupants. They'd never found anything more than a spliff in Casey's bedroom – he was cleverer than that – and besides, Casey senior would have torn him a new one should he ever have stashed gear in the family home. Michael could also count on several willing female volunteers – all promised a bright future – who quite happily secreted his dirty little packages inside their bodies. As far as he was concerned, the stupid bitches were ten a penny and once he'd used them up – or they'd been caught with drugs by the cops – he'd drop them in a heartbeat and easily replace them. He'd fathered a child with at least one of his drug-carrying harem, but hadn't given a toss about such minor inconveniences and had dropped them too. He was slowly but surely turning into a real bastard, was young Michael Casey…

Realising that the key to success in the drug dealing game, hinged upon distancing himself from the dirty work of actually selling his product; he'd employed a steady stream of runners – ferrying little packets from grubby apartments to the occupants of cars waiting below - just as he had done not that long before, in the employ of the Afghan. Dropouts, some as young as thirteen years old - many of whom could scarcely read and write - were, it seemed, in endless supply in the area that he lived and he'd never been short of a runner. The drab, grey high rise blocks, home to countless one parent families with stairwells stinking of urine and the residue of crack; spawned dozens of track suited feral youths all easily impressed by the dealer's flash cars, heavy gold jewellery and fake Rolex or Breitling wrist watches. Who needed education or a job, when even a small time dealer of cannabis could make far more in a day than the cops who tracked him? Working was for mugs in those areas and being caught by the police, an occupational hazard. Of course, maintaining a distance from his little bags of pungent weed hadn't prevented the cops stopping him wherever they'd encountered him, and although their constant harassment did nothing more than disrupt him, until they could pin him down, they'd satisfied themselves with pissing him off. His car had been flagged on the Police National Computer as being worth a stop and wherever he'd been within the boundaries of the Metropolitan police, he was assured of being stopped at least once a day. Casey had learned to be polite and to play the game, and at first, he'd made sure to switch cars regularly. This had worked up to a point, but the leviathan, that was PNC, generally tended to be only a couple of steps behind him. Some cops thrived on gathering and disseminating intelligence, whether it was gleaned from informants, jealous and disgruntled neighbours, home beat cops, or their less respected counterparts; the Police Community Support Officers. The latter, were known affectionately as Blunkett's Bobbies (after the then home secretary who'd come up with the idea as a cost saving exercise) and known not so affectionately as "plastic cops" Actually, some of those PCSOs, whose mandate was to patrol the local council estates and high street shops, were worth their weight in gold when it came to picking up and recording information. It could have been said, with some justification, that there were those among the PCSOs who seemed to spend their every waking moment recording trivial crap, but every now and then a nugget of decent information would emerge, which gave the cops a small but vital head start. Learning from the big boys, Casey junior circumvented the problem of having his cars recognised and stopped, by using rental cars for himself and his runners to drive around in. This had proved to be effective up to a point, but the more switched on and proactive officers, had taken to stopping any car which (a) came back on PNC as a rental, and (b) looked to be driven by "scrotes" There were certain parts of London, where, to a decent officer, certain cars didn't quite fit and certain drivers and their passengers just *looked* like scrotes. Recognising these people couldn't be taught – just learned through experience. There being more ways than one to skin a cat, the more astute boys and girls in blue, up on their law, knew that if a rental car was being driven by any driver other than the one named on the rental agreement, he would be technically committing the crime of "taking and driving away" and TDA, a technicality or not, came under the theft act, thereby rendering the driver liable to arrest and prosecution. The more pedantic among the officers, could also claim that the scrote – as an unauthorised driver - had not only taken the car without permission, but had driven it whilst uninsured. A follow up call to the hire company ensured that the car would be collected and the original hirer blacklisted. Result? Cops 1 Scrotes 0

It had been in one of his rental cars, that Michael – his local supply temporarily suspended after a series informant led police raids – had driven to the unfamiliar territory of north east London and the blot on the landscape that was the notorious Holly Street Estate. Among the decent families struggling through life on the minimum wage, the hulking blocks housed immigrants, families on benefits and more than a few dangerous criminals to whom automatic weapons such as the deadly little MAC -10 were standard issue. The "spray and pray" machine gun, favoured by London gangsters, was originally designed by Gordon B Ingram in 1964 and manufactured by the Military Armament Corporation. It had been the short-range weapon of choice for US Special Forces during the Vietnam War. With its fire rate of 1090 rounds per minute, it was absolutely lethal in confined spaces and had been used to deadly effect not only on the so called "Trident" boroughs of London, but also in the high rise blocks on Casey's home ground of Brentford.

Apart from Holly Street being unfamiliar territory, the sprawling estate, with it's warren-like design – the handiwork of some well meaning and forward thinking architect of the 1960's - was regularly patrolled not only by the response officers of Hackney Borough, but on occasion - due to the nature of some of it's inhabitants - by armed officers from SO19. This increased the risk for Casey of being stopped, but his dwindling supplies had forced the issue, and needs must when the devil drives… He'd also found himself in the unfamiliar position of being alone – he had planned to pick up a damn sight more weed than could be inserted into a female orifice and his usual cohort – the dumb bastard - was answering bail for a public order offence after telling a cop to "go fuck himself" during a cocaine fuelled night out. The offer to replenish his stocks had come with the proviso that he either pick it up that morning or not bother.

Parking his car in the shadow of one of the blocks, he took a precautionary walk around the general area to make sure he hadn't been followed or that the address for his pick up wasn't under obvious observation. Satisfying himself as best as he could, he'd got into the tin box of a lift and punched in the number to take him to the top floor. The grinding, protesting elevator had stopped a couple of times, once to admit a young woman with her pushchair and it's chocolate smeared passenger, and again just before the top, where a wide eyed Somali, his cheeks stuffed hamster-like with *Khat,* had joined them. At the top floor, the stinking lift had disgorged its cargo of single mother hurrying home to catch the latest edition of Jeremy Kyle, the Somali, his mouth dribbling with the juice of *Khat,* and the small time drug dealer from west London.

Rapping his knuckles on the door of the chicken coop that was number 498, Casey was challenged from within by a female's voice asking, "Who is it?" As instructed, feeling slightly ridiculous, he had replied, "Post man" and with a scrape of bolts, he'd been admitted into a surprisingly pleasant and clean apartment. The attractive brunette within, didn't waste time on pleasantries and within ten seconds of his arrival, she'd taken his proffered wad of cash and exchanged it for a cheap rucksack. A cursory examination of the rucksack's contents confirmed that he was now the proud owner of ten blocks of compressed vegetable matter otherwise known as "blue cheese" This latest strain of cannabis, gave even the strongest smelling *skunk* a bad name, but he had to admit, so well had it been packaged, that unless you were a spaniel in the employ of the Metropolitan police, you'd never get a whiff of it. The brunette – chosen for her lack of police record, was lacking in pleasantries and had ushered the stranger out of her neat apartment before he'd realised that the only word he'd spoken had been "postman"

Out on the landing, he'd summoned the ancient lift and watched as the floor numbers flashed up on the filthy screen above its doors. He noticed idly, and with some impatience, that it seemed to stop at just about every floor before it reached the top. When it finally arrived and the doors squealed open, he'd seen two hooded youths inside and wondered idly why they hadn't got out. Thinking "Whatever" Casey junior had joined them in the cramped space that stank of disinfectant. The doors to the elevator closed with a grating protest and Michael and the companions forced upon him, began their descent. His mind focused on getting the hell out of the unfamiliar shit hole, and despite being a streetwise criminal, who was normally attuned to danger, he had embraced the English attitude of not only refraining from speech with strangers, but studiously ignoring them. In doing so, he'd missed the obvious – he'd missed the fact that youth (a) had a knife tucked into the waistband of his hipster jeans and he'd also missed the fact that youth (b) had a canister of CS spray in his right hand, which was stuffed into the pocket of his hooded top. The first Casey had known of his mistake, was when youth (b) had suddenly and without warning sprayed him full in the face with the CS spray that was readily available in Europe, but that was classed as a firearm in Britain. Choking on the spray, tears involuntarily streaming down his face and snot running from his nose, Casey had put up a gallant defence of his merchandise. So gallant had his defence been, that youth (a) had seen no option other than to plunge what was an ordinary and unglamorous six inch vegetable knife into the chest of the out of town dealer; piercing first his heart and then deflating a lung with the second strike. Ripping the rucksack from the shoulders of the now gasping for life west London dealer, the hood rats had exited the stinking lift at the next floor and descended the remainder of the floors by way of the stairs. Reaching the bottom, they'd disappeared into the rat runs of the South Kilburn estate before jumping into the anonymity of a double decker bus. With no other call on the lift bearing the dying Casey, it had run it's full course to the ground floor. When its protesting doors had opened, they did so to reveal Michael Casey, small time dealer of cannabis, and son of the failed post office robber, gurgling and burping crimson bubbles onto his fake Gucci shirt.

The Polish woman, on her way to her job as a hairdresser, had screamed, when exiting her ground floor flat, the elevator doors had opened to reveal the dying dealer. Transfixed, she'd stood in shock as the doors closed yet again, taking the lift's gruesome cargo back upwards; this time to the fifth floor, where it had been summoned by and old boy and his dog. It had been tragicomic – the lift that morning – up and down the floors like some macabre pass the parcel, Casey had spent the last minutes of his life shuttling between the floors of that God forsaken tower block, his life force ebbing away with every level. By the time the police had arrived, the elevator had been thick with blood, Casey was long dead, and the hood rats; who'd been acting on the tip off that a stranger, unfamiliar with the way of Holly street, was about to leave with a decent stash, were already in Tottenham, handing over their ill gotten gains to the guy who'd tipped them off and set up the fateful Casey deal in the first place.

CHAPTER 11
Revelations

Back in that place Jake Turner was feeling a little odd, couldn't quite put his finger on it, but his body ached and he'd begun to feel uncomfortable, it was almost as if the fug of Pethidine sedation was beginning to wear off, leaving him feeling well – actually, quite normal. For normal, read, the back of his head had developed a dull, nagging toothache kind of pain, and he felt the same kind of pain in his left arm just above the elbow and in his right ankle. Nothing desperate, just discomfort. Sitting on his bench, he felt as though he'd been perched there forever, but unlike the "all's well with the world" feelings he'd experienced when he first arrived, he'd begun to feel twitchy; that restless leg sort of thing, like he'd felt back in the world, during a wasted Sunday on the couch after a heavy drinking session. Along with these earthly sensations, there was a muted roar in his eardrums; not unlike the sound of a seashell held up to one's ear. As a child, Jake had played with his grandmother's collection of exotic shells, the larger of which he'd "listened" to while sprawled on the fluffy white rug in front of her fire. When fascinated, he'd asked his gran where the noise had been coming from; the old lady had smiled and told him that it was the sound of the sea. Despite his bodily discomfort and the irritating sound in his ears, he smiled at the memory of his old Nan and her silly stories.

Getting up from his bench, he decided to seek relief from his aching head and limbs by going for a walk, and set off along the infinite hallway apace. He had the notion that he would keep walking until he reached the end of that place. The perpetual bright light, which up to now hadn't bothered him, now started to aggravate his headache and as he walked, he endeavoured to find some place that might have been in some kind of shadow. There were, it seemed, some corridors, which led off the main thoroughfare, all of which appeared to have no real purpose. He explored a couple of them, but although they were of varying lengths, they all ended in dead ends, were deserted, and were just as illuminated as the rest of the place. He persisted nonetheless, and walked down each one in the hope of finding something – anything to stimulate his ever-increasing curiosity. He reflected idly, that up until now, when the feeling of wellbeing had begun to wear off to be replaced with restlessness; he hadn't been driven by the need to do anything more than sit on his bench with the odd perambulation and interaction with his fellow dead. After what seemed like an age, Jake Turner, by now resigned to finding nothing more than another dead end, turned right down yet another corridor. Before long, it became obvious that this particular corridor was different to all the rest. It felt colder; and the further he traveled along its length, the colder it became – not only colder – but also dimmer. Eventually reaching the end, he could just about make out some kind of door looming out of the gloom. It was a heavy-duty door and was constructed from a material, which he didn't recognise as either wood or plastic – it reminded Jake of a cell door in the custody area of the police stations he'd brought many a prisoner to – with the exception, that there was no wicket incorporated from which the duty gaoler could look through and check on the occupant's activities. Walking up to the studded, fortified door, he touched it before putting an ear to it and then recoiling from its icy feel. He wasn't sure if his mind was playing tricks on him, but could have sworn that he could hear shouts and groans coming from within.

Tentatively, he pushed at the door and was somewhat surprised when it had swung open with the minimum of effort – almost as though it had been hydraulically assisted, like some door to a public building back in the world; designed for the disabled to access with a push of a giant button. Immediately it had opened, the shouts and groans, which Jake had thought he'd heard from the other side, were confirmed. It looked and sounded like a Crimean War field hospital from some black and white film about Florence Nightingale back in the world. Peering into the gloom – Turner –whose whole body screamed "Get the fuck out of here" was drawn inexplicably inside. The floor was littered with humanity; some sitting, their legs drawn up to their bodies while rocking in the manner of lunatics in an asylum, while others, their pathetic frames wracked with pain, had screwed up their bodies into a ball, like some child's first attempt at papier mache. Some of the inhabitants of that dreadful room were on their hands and knees in the foetal position, with yet more, simply flat on their backs. Regardless of their bodily position, all had one thing in common – they all appeared to be in pain and cried out for deliverance from their agony.

Jake didn't know what had drawn him ever further into that dreadful room, but something akin to an invisible force had compelled him to continue ever further into the depths of the place. Suddenly, despite the temperature of that awful chamber, he heard something that chilled him to the bone.

'Jake – is that you old mate?' The voice, riddled with pain cut him to the quick.

'Len?'

The voice continued, wheezing, hoarse, and laden with catarrh:

'Help me Jakey, I'm fuckin' dying here!'

'Where are you mate?'

Not waiting for an answer and confused by Lenny Roberts' announcement that he was dying when he was already long dead, Jake sought out the source of his old friend's voice from among the cacophony of misery. Walking towards the back of the room, he came across Len, his body screwed ball-like, up against a wall. Like a broken doll, Lenny Roberts – victim of a tragic car crash over thirty years before, unwrapped his arms from the ball that had become his body and looked up at his old army mate. His face was white as chalk and Jake could see blood running freely from his nose – the same nose that in repose in the front room of his parent's house, all those years ago; had been stuffed by the undertaker with cotton wool, stemming the blood and thin bodily fluids that in death had trickled unhindered from the boy's nostrils as he'd lain in the casket.

Dropping to one knee, Turner bent over his friend's pain ridden body. Now that he was close to him, he became aware of an overwhelming smell, which appeared to hang, cloudlike above his stricken mate. The smell was that of petrol, mixed with the sweet stench of hydraulic fluid and engine oil. Strangely, Lenny Roberts was dressed in clothes from the 1980's. Jake was pretty sure he hadn't been dressed like that the last time he'd seen him, when he'd playfully taunted him about his relationship with the junkie girl, Sarah Tunney. He couldn't have sworn to it, but then again, he'd have been hard pressed to swear to anything right now. Was he dreaming? Had he actually left his bench and traveled along the expanse of white to this grim charnel house – or was this another Pethidine moment? Lenny – his voice feeble and barely audible shook him out of his stupefaction. His hands clutching weakly at Jake's sleeve. He whispered:

'Jakey – you still there mate?' Accepting that this was no dream, Turner sat in the gloom, and on the cold floor, cradled his old army friend's head.

'I'm here Len'

'Glad you could make it Jakey' Then with the weakest of smiles – 'I think I've just crashed my fuckin' car!'

There it was, a spark of the character he'd once known - a glimmer of a spark, like that from a sodden flint – but a spark nonetheless. And then he was gone; the spark that had momentarily danced in his dull eyes doused, his body limp, his friend no more. Just as he'd vanished from Jake's life all those years ago, he'd gone again and Turner relived the anguish - except this time it was different. Icy cold fingers of realisation seeped cruelly into his heart – If Lenny Roberts had been dead before and yet "alive" in this place and he'd just "died" again – what the fuck was going on? Was this the way it was going to be for him – for all those he'd met here? Would they all, at a time of some unseen beings' choice, drag themselves to that dreadful chamber and relive the pain and agony that had brought them here to this place? And then what? Somewhere else? An eternal carousel of misery? It was too much for Jake to take in; he was confused and frightened. Gently releasing Lenny's head and laying him down, he got back to his feet and waded his way back through the writhing humanity of that dreadful room. Pushing open the heavy door, he fled in tears back to the sanctity of the bright light. As he walked back the way he'd come, the pain in his ankle increased in its intensity making him hobble the rest of the way to his bench. 'Where' he thought grimly 'Is the bloody Pethidine when you need it?'

Clinging to the sense of familiarity that was *his* bench – his safe mooring in that great expanse of white - he approached his familiar seat, but could see that in his absence, someone else had occupied it. Initially he thought "Bloody cheek!" but upon seeing the interloper, his attitude softened at once. Curled up on his bench and fast asleep, was Sarah Tunney, and although he was heartened to see the girl he'd developed a soft spot for; he was loathe to wake her, and instead, sat himself down on the floor in front of her slumbering form. Presently, his ass became numb on the hard floor, and shifting position to get comfortable, he spotted something shiny underneath his bench just beyond where Sarah's fingers trailed the floor. Jake reached for it and as he did so, assumed that it must have fallen from the girl's hand, relaxed as it was in sleep. Getting his fingertips to it, he slid the object out, and examined it. Immediately, Turner recognised it to be an old fashioned Polaroid photograph with its typical black backing paper, and with curiosity taking over, he turned it over in his hand. At some point, there appeared to have been some writing at the bottom of the photo, but time and handling had made it illegible. Never mind what the inscription had once been; it was the actual faded image – yellowed by time – which sent a jolt through his body. Jake time flashed...

His stay in Hounslow, the convenient stopover for the south east leg of the KAPE tour; had been dull in the extreme – not much business for the strutting squaddies there – just the odd ancient Ghurkha reminiscing over days past, and the white teenage yob element from the estates of Feltham - all swaggering bravado under their skinhead hairdos. The boredom had been punctuated only by the off duty excitement of a young man making forays into the neighbouring towns of Richmond and Kingston. There he'd joined the night club queues of young bucks trying to act sober enough to get past the meathead, steroid pumped, doormen in their bomber jackets and self important earpieces. Once inside - full of overpriced lager and doused with the cheap cologne dispensed by the pushy African toilet attendants ("No splash – no gash") – he'd been free to sample the delights, and thinly veiled promises of the scantily clad, high heeled local girls, who gyrated on the darkened dance floor within.

It had been during one such drink fuelled night, early into his stay at the cavalry barracks, that he'd been chatted up by a local girl – not his usual type – a bit too forward and *chavvy* for his liking, and the girl did like a drink; but there had been something about her, and he'd found himself spending more and more time with her. He liked the way that she clung to him and made him feel special. After a couple of dates, he'd sneaked her over the camp perimeter wall and into his barrack room. They'd had wonderful booze fuelled sex and he had to admit, that she'd taught him a thing or two. If not in love with the girl, he'd certainly fallen in lust with her! It had been her idea – the photo – seeing Jake's newly bought Polaroid camera hanging by it's strap in his room, she'd grabbed it, giggling and got him to take some pictures of her in compromising positions. Those cheeky pictures had kept him warm on many a cold German sentry duty! When he looked into the little window showing the film counter and saw that they'd used up all but one on shots of her naked body, he'd pulled her back onto the bed and under the covers, where, faces pressed together, and smiling up towards the camera lens, he'd taken one last snap of them both. Jake had kept the saucy ones and she'd kept the smiley one of them both. At the end of his short stay in the borough of Dick Turpin, he'd continued his journey northward with the rest of the KAPE team, and although he'd not forgotten the girl from Hounslow, he'd had to admit, it was more a case of fondness than love, and he'd moved on in that free spirited way of the soldier, to pastures new.

It wasn't long after his return to Germany, that he was sent with his regiment to the Falkland Islands, to provide air defence protection to the huge construction project that was to be the new Mount Pleasant airfield. After the Argentineans had been defeated and driven from the islands, the politicians and defence mandarins back at Whitehall, could ill afford to leave the islands as undefended as they had been before the invasion. Port Stanley airfield was deemed unfit for purpose, and at great expense, the new military airfield at Mount Pleasant had been conceived and authorised. Jake had been there three months when he'd received what amounted to manna from heaven to a soldier posted to the furthest outposts of what was left of the empire. The manna came in the form of the rare and coveted bluey, a flimsy self-sealing blue coloured letter – free to send and receive via the British Forces Post Office. Out of all the postings at that time – the Falklands was the furthest a bluey had to travel and was probably the most welcome.

The letter, addressed to Bombardier Turner. J at BFPO 666 (The military postal code for the Falkland Islands) hadn't been in the manna category. God knows how the girl from Hounslow had managed to get his address, but the contents of that particular bluey hadn't been welcome news at all. It informed him of the earth shattering news, that on the night back in his barrack room, where they'd giggled over the girl's raunchy Polaroid pictures, when they'd argued playfully over who would sleep in the wet patch – on that night – he'd impregnated her. The letter continued, that he was to be a father before the year was out. Turner hadn't been ready for fatherhood and in the style typical of a transient young man; he'd blanked the letter, blanked the girl and blanked his responsibilities. It hadn't been until he'd been much older with a daughter through wedlock, that he'd given the girl from Hounslow proper and wistful consideration; but of course, with all contact long since lost and a sea of bitterness dividing them, he'd shrugged off the notion of ever seeing the girl and the child he had fathered in the damp barrack room so long before.

Back in that place, a million miles from the cavalry barracks in Hounslow and an eternity since he'd received that fateful bluey, Jake Turner sat bolt upright. Christ! That picture – that was young Jake Turner smiling back at him from his old barrack room bed – he even recognised the cheap duvet cover he'd proudly bought from IKEA with the "oh so grown up" Latin verses scrawled in gold over it's parchment-like design. He remembered with a wistful smile, the Playboy pictures on the pin board above his head, and memories came flooding back, unbidden and swirling like a whirlpool in his head. The other person in the photo – the cute and grinning female – that's what had freaked him out; not only did he remember the "good time girl", who'd posed raunchily for him all those years ago, but looking at Sarah sleeping on the bench above him, he was stunned to see that she was the spitting image of the woman in the Polaroid, now smiling up at him from the battered old picture in his shaking hand. Could the junkie really be the child that in the ignorant arrogance of youth, he'd cruelly abandoned? Could she have been the one left by him, to the fate of growing up in the shit hole borough of Dick Turpin, destined to become yet another statistic of absentee fathers untraced by the State? With a heavy heart, suddenly laden with guilt, Jake surmised that she had to be one and the same - yet another dirty little secret, dragged back up from his past to confront him. Still holding the faded evidence of neglect in his hand, tears rolling down his face, he knelt over Sarah – *his* Sarah – and gently stroked her hair. Coming slowly to, Jake's daughter, looked around in some confusion, before moving her head away from his touch. Sleepily she said:

'Oh, there you are, I wondered where you'd got to, what's up?'
Then seeing his tear streaked face, she laughed before continuing;
'Didn't think cops were capable of crying'

Sitting up, she felt around in the back pocket of her jeans before standing up and checking the bench on which she'd been sleeping. A look of mild panic pricking her emerald eyes, she got onto her hands and knees and searched under the seat. A weight of guilt gnawing at his guts, he held out the Polaroid – 'You looking for this Sarah?'

Relief flooded the girl's eyes; she smiled, and Sarah Tunney's smile was identical to that of the woman captured in the picture of the couple on the barrack room bed.

'Thanks Jake – thought I'd lost it' Averting his gaze, he asked: 'What year were you born Sarah?'

Shooting the older man a quizzical look, she hesitated before replying.

'1984 – why'd you ask?'

Putting an arm around her shoulder, he gently guided her back onto his bench before joining her there.

'That photo Sarah – what did the inscription used to say?'

'Stop being weird Jake – you're not a cop any more you know and besides, its personal and I'm not sure it's any of your business!'

'Please Sarah, do an old man a favour it's important'

Looking at Turner – the only man ever to have shown her any warmth, with a "for fuck's sake" the junkie from Hounslow relented.

'If you must know – Mr PC Plod – it used to say: "Having a laugh with soldier boy" So what's it to you?'

His voice trembling with emotion, Jake asked the one question that would confirm him to be the girl's father – not that he had any doubt – it was almost as though he was seeking to prolong the decision of whether to tell her or not. How would she take it? Would his shocking revelation result in her slapping him? Storming off never to be seen again? Now he'd found her, he didn't think he could have coped with losing the daughter he'd had to die to find.

'The woman in that picture Sarah – is she your mother? Because if she is, I have to tell you, that the boy lying next to her, the boy who didn't have the guts to face her when she got into trouble, the bastard that disappeared without lifting a finger to help bring you up? That bastard Sarah – was – is me…' There, he'd said it, for better or for worse, he'd made his sordid confession, not to a priest, but to his own flesh and blood…

The girl stared at him slack jawed, and then she looked at the photo and stared at him again this time with anger pin pointing her pupils. Jumping suddenly to her feet, hands on hips, she let her father have both barrels.

'OK, so let's get this straight – not only am I a fuckin' dead crack head, but I've ended up *here* – wherever the fuck *here* is - sharing my afterlife, *whatever* the fuck that is, with a bastard copper who couldn't keep his prick in his fuckin' pants!'

Jake rose and tried to put his hands on Sarah's shoulders, but with a 'Don't fuckin' touch me' his distraught daughter pushed him back onto his bench – *hard.*

'You've every reason to hate me Sarah…' he began

'Yes I fuckin' well have!' she spat back. 'Now leave me the fuck alone!'

Turning angrily on her heel, Sarah Tunney daughter of Jake Turner stalked away leaving him sitting on that loathsome bench, his stomach like a stone.

In another far-flung corner of that vast white and sterile place, Damien Jones, the fitness instructor, cruelly taken away from the world by congenital defects; who'd allied himself with the squaddies and their Rupert from Afghanistan had sought a temporary reprieve from their banter and gone walkabout. It wasn't as though he hadn't enjoyed their camaraderie, just that he wanted some downtime. He'd begun to feel drowsy again, rubbernecking, his chin bouncing off his chest every few minutes, and wanted to do something, anything to shake off the foggy feeling of inactivity. Wandering the concourse, Damien came across a group of men huddled in earnest conversation. They all bore the same characteristics – pride and a ramrod appearance. The oddity was, that although they were dressed in some antiquated frogman-like attire, they were all wearing the green beret of the Royal Marines atop their close- cropped heads. To a man, the group were either unaware of his presence, or else feigned indifference. Captivated by the men, Damien hovered nearby and listened to them as they talked proudly of Operation Frankton and seemed to be reminiscing about a submarine - HMS Tuna - in the reverential manner one might have referred to a favourite aunt. It wasn't until one of their number suddenly guffawed: 'Cockleshell heroes? – Can you believe that? Heroes – that's what they called us back home – cockleshell bloody heroes! What a load of bollocks!' the men roared with laughter, before falling silent, each immersed in his own thoughts.

The very words "cockleshell heroes" ran through young Damien Jones, instantly reviving his boyhood obsession with all things Royal Marine. Hadn't his mother sat him on her knee and recounted the bravery of her father and all the other ill-fated cockleshell boys fifty years earlier? Of course, his grandfather Ernie had perished at the hands of the Germans many years before his daughter had been old enough to marry and later give birth to his grandchild Damien; and while his grandson had had the advantage of knowing Ernie's history inside out, Ernie had been long gone by the time Damien had arrived. Young Jonesy had one distinct advantage over his dead predecessor though; and that had been pictorial evidence, and lots of it. Grandad in his dress blues, medals gleaming in the sun on the parade ground, grandad in his frogman outfit, grandad, face smeared with camouflage cream, woolly commando hat on, paddling a canvas canoe, and yet more in civilian clothes, his square jaw clean shaven and jutting proud at his wedding.

The gravelly, yet jovial tones cut through Jonesy's childhood reflections.

'Ere, young 'un, what you lookin' at?'

The men, as one, turned to look at Damien and he suddenly felt guilty, like a snooper, eavesdropping on a private conversation.

'Er...' he began. The gravelly voice continued. 'Don't be shy young fella, come over here'

Looking nervously in the direction of that voice, his heart skipped a beat, as he recognised, without a shred of doubt, his maternal grandfather Ernie Bishop, late of his Majesty's Royal Marines.

'Grandad...?' he began, feeling like a kid.

'Bloody hell Bish' exclaimed one of the group – 'Someone your missus doesn't know about?'

The rest of the bootnecks fell about laughing before one of their number beckoned Damien over. Sat in their midst, Damien felt instantly at home. Gravel voice patted him on the back. 'What's all this grandad shit about young 'un?'

Regaining his confidence, the gym instructor looked into the eyes of the man he'd hero worshipped as a kid.

'Your daughter Elsie' he managed to blurt out hoarsely – I'm Elsie's son – the grandson you never knew!'

The group fell quiet then, all bravado and banter temporarily shelved in favour of a respectful silence. Ernie's weather-beaten face took on the look of both pride and sorrow. Looking at the grandson he never got to see back in the world, he regained his composure and for appearances sake – in front of his hard-bitten mates – slapped his thigh in the manner of an old time Hollywood buccaneer and bellowed:

'Of course you're my grandson! Look what a handsome cove he is muckers!'

Much to the amusement of his shipmates, Marine Bishop sidled up close to Damien and playfully thrust his head next to that of his grandson so as to be cheek to cheek with his blood relative, before inviting complimentary comparison from the other cockleshellers. Feeling the older man's leathery skin next to his own, Damien smelled that old familiar smell – the smell that had been released into his room every time he'd opened the old medal box in his bedroom back in the world. The briny, yet sweet tang of the sea was once again in his nostrils, and young Jonesy felt content. He'd met his childhood hero, and now happily basked in the attention of grandad Bishop and his ill-fated fellow marines from HMS Tuna, who had moved a respectful distance from the two, allowing their privacy. The young gym instructor and his marine idol shared a seat in that place and talked of war, family, and the modern world his grandfather had never known. The proud marine, cut down in his prime forty years before Damien was even a twinkle in his mother's eye, related the horrors of war to his attentive grandson. He relived the fateful mission – his last – and the one that was to take his life; the mission impossible to the French harbour that had been crawling with the coalscuttle helmets of occupying Nazis. In return, young Jonesy told Ernie all about his own attempts to become a marine and about how he'd fallen at the hurdle that had exposed his defects. He'd felt ashamed and embarrassed to tell his warrior grandad about how he'd failed to make the grade, but his mother's father had reassured him, saying how proud he was of his grandson; how the real life horror of war wasn't in the least bit glamorous and served to do little more than cream off the youth of a country, before cruelly laying waste to them. Damien told his grandad all about his work at

111

the Parkside Club, and all about the girl; Rita from the shantytowns of Brazil, who'd been the last person he'd seen and touched before his young life had ended at around the same age that grandad Bishop had died. This revelation had the marine in fits of laughter and between the giggles and the thigh slapping, he'd made a comparison:

'So, young Damien – I died fucking the German navy up and you died fucking a Brazilian – you randy little bugger!'

Slapping him on the back, and pulling him to his feet, he jumped onto the bench and turned to his shipmates. 'Muckers!' he announced with a bow – 'I give you my grandson Damien, and do hereby induct him into the club of dead fuckers! Here's to women everywhere – Brazilian or otherwise - and here's to the German navy – fucked by the cockleshell heroes!'

Glowing with pride and with the raucous whoops and shouts of his grandfather's band of brothers ringing in his ears, Jonesy sat back down. Suddenly he felt tired, his sight grew dim, and his vision became tunnel like. Not wanting this moment of brotherhood to end, he battled sleep, but there, on his bench, surrounded by his boyhood heroes, he succumbed to the weight of his eyelids.

Damien came to the sounds of bored banter; the type of banter normally the reserve of men cooped up together in hardship; the banter of the military or cops in a riot van; the piss taking, the farting and belching. Glad to find the cockleshellers hadn't left while he'd been sleeping, he opened his eyes to find that although he was indeed still in the company of military men, their WW2 uniforms had been replaced by modern desert camouflage smocks and the faces were those not of Ernie Bishop's band of brothers, but those of the Rupert, Pat and Jim. The banter included him, the minute he opened his eyes:

'Oh' said Jim 'I see sleeping beauty's back with us then!'

'Yeah' laughed Pat, 'Except I didn't see no handsome prince kissing him – unless you count the Rupert – bet *he's* got some royal princely connection with that plum in his mouth!'

Damien laughed weakly; he was still trying to figure out the whole grandad thing. Had he dreamt the whole episode, or had his childhood idol really been here, in *this place*? One thing he knew for sure, the encounter had felt real to him and he still glowed from the experience of meeting Ernie and the men from HMS Tuna. They'd made him feel six feet tall and given him a feeling of belonging, of pride. His mother's father - apparition or otherwise - had seemed genuinely proud of him and that was priceless. Raising his hand in a salute, he murmured 'Wherever you are grandad – thank you, and God bless…'

CHAPTER TWELVE
The Charnel House

I had a little Sorrow,
Born of a little Sin,
I found a room all damp with gloom
And shut us all within;
And, "Little Sorrow, weep," said I,
"And, Little Sin, pray God to die,
And I upon the floor will lie
And think how bad I've been!" (From Edna ST. Vincent Millay's The
Penitent*)*

Jake Turner, still in a state of abject misery since his disastrous
revelation of fatherhood to Sarah Tunney, sat on his bench feeling
sorry for himself. His head was killing him and he could only walk
with difficulty; such was the nagging pain in his right ankle. The
discomfort in his left arm had led him to utilise an old army first aid
trick; that of rolling up his pullover from the bottom up, to encase
the lower part of his arm in the thick wool and so keep it immobile.
By holding the stricken limb close to his body and using his pullover
as a makeshift sling, he found some relief from the dull throbbing
sensation, the agony and fire, which no form of drug – not even
Pethidine – could quench. Coupled with the distraction of his painful
extremities, was the roaring in his ears. No longer at the innocent
level of his gran's seashells, it had increased in intensity so as to be
almost unbearable. His sense of humour hadn't completely deserted
him though, and grimacing, he made fun of his predicament:
'You're falling to bits old mate, get a grip!'
He wondered if the daughter he'd never known back in the world,
and only got to know in death, would relent and speak to him or
indeed, whether he would ever see her again. He hoped that in time,
he'd be given the opportunity to in some way explain why he had
abandoned her, why he'd torn up the bluey brought to his lonely
Falklands outpost by helicopter all those years ago. And if she did
ever seek him out again, how would he tell her that her mother had
been just another conquest; another notch on the bedpost of a young
"devil may care" squaddie passing through town and her mother's
life? Turner was shaken from his self-indulgent reflections by the

gruff voice of his dad's old mate:

'Jakey! How's it hanging?'

Looking up at Harry Thomas, the old medic who'd left him with the dogleg scar on his foot after his mother's frustrated jar-throwing episode, Jake managed a weak smile.

'Hello mate, I'm feeling like shit if I'm honest'

The old corporal sat down next to him and as he did, Jake noticed that he was wheezing, his short breaths coming fast and shallow, his face ashen.

'You don't sound so good yourself!'

'That, Jakey, is 'cos I'm an old man who died from smoking too many cigarettes and putting away the equivalent of an independent Scottish distillery! What's your excuse? And what have you done to your arm?'

'I'm in bits Harry, my ankle feels as if it's being cut into with a hacksaw, I can't move my arm, and some bastard's running their train set through my head!'

Harry the Dog smiled mischievously. 'Apart from that you're alright then?'

'Same old Harry eh?'

'Of course, what else is there? – Truth be known Jakey, I'm feeling pretty fucked up too you know. I've been coughing up blood since the last time I saw you and my lungs are on fire – guess we're both for the knackers' yard eh?'

They lapsed into silence, the old medic and his friend's son, each lost in their thoughts and the nagging worry about what came next. It hadn't seemed too bad at first – their arrival in this place, but Harry was no longer in a position to go to his medical centre cabinet and fish out the drugs that could have sent them both to a merciful and pain-free opiate heaven. It was Jake who broken the silence first:

'Harry?'

'Yes mate?'

'You ever have any kids?'

His old friend laughed, 'Only six – why?'

'It's just that…' The younger man trailed off, not really sure where he was going with this.

'Go on Jakey – you've got a daughter haven't you?'

'I have Harry, and another one besides; one that I knew about, but had nothing to do with…'

'Oh, I see… ' Putting a paternal arm around Jake's shoulders, the old medic encouraged him to continue. 'Mate, we've all got skeletons in our closets; things we aren't proud of, it's the stuff of life Jakey, but why now, why bring it up here in *this place*?'

Turner looked at the floor. 'Because she's here Harry – here among us – here among the dead where she shouldn't be. I mean, we all have to die, but where's the fairness in a young girl being here so many years before her time?'

The old medic hugged Jake close, 'Life's not fair Jakey, never has been, but what's this about another daughter – did you know about her? How did you find out?'

'Oh I knew about her Dog, just chose to ignore her existence; too busy gallivanting around the world getting drunk and shagging any female daft enough to give me the time of day!'

'Ah, the ignorance of youth' rejoined Harry sagely. 'It happens mate; it's all very well having a girl in every port – and believe me – I did, but it's only when you're older, when those chickens of conscience come home to roost, that you start to reflect on things that you wish you'd done better. I've got flocks of those fuckers – chickens I mean! It's life Jakey and what's done is done, no point beating yourself up over it. Easy for me to say I know, but you're not the first and you won't be the last…'

'I know you're right Dog, but why did I have to leave it until I'm dead to try and make amends?'

The old boy looked quizzical.

'But, how can you Jake, you're here in this place and your little girl's back in the world, probably made a good life for herself'

'Weren't you listening to me Harry? She's right here with us somewhere in this fuckin' palace of light, a junkie dead by her own hand, clutching an old Polaroid of her bastard dad! I've met her and spilled my guts to the poor girl and not surprisingly, she wants nothing more to do with me!'

Harry gave Jake a sympathetic squeeze; 'She'll come round mate, in time'

In the depths of despair, much as he valued the Dog's company, Jake was inconsolable. 'In *time* Harry?' he repeated 'Just how much *time* do you think we've got? Eternity? Five minutes? What?'

116

His dad's old mate didn't reply, truth be known, he didn't really know what to say, and besides, he wasn't feeling too clever himself. His throat felt as though he'd been gargling with broken glass and his chest, as though it were in the grip of one of those ancient presses he'd seen the Maltese farmers use to extract the meagre trickle of oil offered up by the puny local olives. The old man and his young friend sat in silence, each lost in thought and propping each other up like human bookends.

Not far away, Jake's daughter Sarah, encountered the bastard again and he didn't seem as cocky as he'd been the last time she had seen him. He was half sitting, half lying on the floor, wheezing and gasping for breath. Tiny flecks of foamy blood were on his face, which looked waxen; she saw the hollow stare of near death in the bastard's eyes and looking down at him, she felt nothing – no hatred – no sympathy – nothing. Her hand fluttered subconsciously to her neck, the side where the artery ran, which back in the world, she'd slashed open, bringing her young life to a violent and untimely end. Here, in this place, there was no pain, no wound, and no scar, but unbidden, her fingers scratched at an itch where the life-ending cut had been made – just an itch – nothing more. Passing the bastard by, she felt numb, her mind still in turmoil from the cop's confession. The anger still simmered, but seeing the bastard again had made her think about the unborn child she'd force-fed crack to, the embryo of a tiny person – *her* tiny person - who'd had no choice in the matter of whether it lived or died; the baby she had never got to hold, the baby that she'd killed with one slash of the craft knife. Sarah imagined the gruesome spectacle of her baby gasping for life in her dead and shrivelled womb, like a tropical fish flapping around, on the carpet having made its bid for freedom only to discover the harsh reality of being out of it's warm and watery environment. She thought about her unborn child clinging vainly to existence as its mother's worthless life had ebbed away. Was she that dissimilar to her father – the cop, Turner? At least he hadn't killed her – maybe not having a father had made her into the junkie that she had been? Or maybe she'd have taken that path anyway – the rebellious path of a cop's kid. Whatever, it had made her think, think about abandonment and which scenario was worse; a young soldier with his life before him, trapped by a loose squaddie groupie who'd got pregnant because she drank too much and had been too stupid to use contraception? Or a dumb junkie bitch, who when the going had got tough, had chosen the selfish option, that of killing herself and her unborn baby? She would never know whether her child could forgive her, but could she forgive her long lost father? She didn't have the answers, here in this place, didn't know what she thought or felt anymore. She did know one thing though, and that was that none of it seemed fair.

'Yeah' she muttered – *I'm* the bitch who murdered her own child, never gave it a chance, and *he's* the bastard who screwed my mum and fucked off - Life's not fair Sarah Tunney, and then you die…'

Not that far away from where Sarah tried to make sense of it all, the squaddies, their young lives snatched away by a crude Taliban IED in the opium fields of Afghanistan, were uncharacteristically, in a mood of contrition. Pat and Jim had ceased to blame their Rupert for the predicament they now found themselves in and had closed ranks. Expressions of physical pain had clouded their hitherto bright young eyes and they had welcomed the Rupert quite literally into their fold. Pulling him up from the bench opposite, Jim sat the Rupert down between himself and Pat, and the three of them linked arms. Jim hadn't known what had prompted this display of kindness, the crossing of the officer/grunt divide – it had just felt natural, and sitting their like conjoined triplets, they sought comfort from one another, comfort from the pain they had started to suffer. The unspoken pact passed wordlessly between them, was that they'd endure the pain together. Gone was the banter, the blame and recriminations; they were now one - three brothers in arms; three brothers in the camouflage uniforms which reflected the barren, godforsaken colour and pattern of that unconquerable land the soldiers of the Queen referred to as "Afghan" – together we stand - divided we fall…

Sitting next to the latest generation of squaddies, whose country's politicians – seemingly ignorant of history - had sent them yet again into the land of the archaic tribesman in the skewed belief that such a place could be brought into the fold of the European model, sat Damien Jones. Grandson of a hero from another time and place, a time when wars were worth fighting, young Damien, former personal trainer to the rich and bored housewives of north London, felt like an outcast. The soldiers he'd put through their paces earlier were now lethargic and, it seemed, with no further need of his services. They appeared to be in pain, which they suffered with the fortitude of fighting men, and as for Damien, he was ignored. Still flushed with pride after the dreamlike encounter with his grandfather, he too was beginning to succumb to the lethargy of the place. Truth be known, he was feeling pretty ropey himself, he'd begun to suffer from heartburn, and his brow was beaded with cold sweat. The young man's cocky vitality – envy of his fellow instructors at the Parkside Club – was beginning to ebb away and he felt powerless to stop it. Despite his earlier elation of meeting the cockleshell heroes, Jonesy now felt like an outsider, an intruder in the closed world of the IED victims from Afghanistan - *persona non grata.* Getting to his feet, he left their closed circle and trudged wearily off into the light in the vain hope of rediscovering his mother's father and the camaraderie of the doomed men from HMS Tuna.

Feeling an inexplicable urge to rise from his bench, Jake Turner disentangled himself from the snoring Harry Thomas; his bookend companion, and set off along the bright and interminable corridor, which seemed to stretch into blinding infinity. He couldn't fathom what the draw was, but on and on he went, one painful step at a time, dragging his useless leg behind him, his slung arm firing spasms of pain through his broken body with each faltering step he took. He didn't encounter anyone along the way, but even if he had, and they had spoken to him, he wouldn't have been able to hear a word; so loud had the roaring, rushing sound in his ears become. Jake couldn't have said how long his pain wracked walk had taken, but in time, he came to the familiar turn in the corridor, the turning which brought him before the heavy door to that dreadful room – the room where he'd held his old mate Lenny Roberts as he'd died for the second time. That awful chamber of death – real death – that of gone forever with no coming back - ever. No fanfare, no grieving relatives and friends, no wake, no fluffy clouds and definitely no angel's harps. Just an agonising death and a ticket to who knew where…

Trance-like and unable to prevent his urge to continue, Turner hobbled painfully up to the door, and reaching it, he pushed on it.

It opened with the same hydraulic-like ease as before, and as it swung smoothly closed behind him, he peered into the dimly lit chamber. That vile room reeked of death, the same disgusting, yet sweet smell of death that had assailed his nostrils on the many occasions when as a policeman, he'd been first to the scene of a rotting corpse; the worldly owner of which, had given up on their selfish world and ended it all with a length of rope, a bottle of pills or a razor. Back there, in the world, the dead bodies had been stiff, still and silent, but here in this place, this charnel house, the barely alive had already began to stink. The stench of death mingled with the warm metallic smell of recently butchered bodies, like that of an old-fashioned sawdust strewn butcher's shop. That smell, the smell of freshly butchered human beings, emanated from the victims of explosions, brave military men and women sent into combat by a government which feigned sadness at their deaths when interviewed on the news broadcasts; yet did little, if anything, to bring the boys and girls back home from their oil-greedy and futile wars. Their broken bodies shredded by crude fertiliser IED's, in far off foreign lands, they lay screaming in pain, dying and surrounded by their own limbs, torn from camouflage clad torsos, still steaming on the floor, and arranged around them like some macabre jigsaw puzzle with no solution.

By now, Jake Turner, once proud member of Her Majesty's Armed Forces and Constable of the Metropolitan police, was feeling weak as a kitten. Crawling on his hands and knees through the morass of human misery, he sought out his own space. Almost blind with pain, he bumped into an inert form, which mumbled incomprehensibly to him. In vain, his ears filled with the tumultuous roar of an ungodly express train, he drew his head close to the source of the mumbling. Still on all fours, he sensed rather than heard, a shallow gasping sound. Jake put an ear to what materialised out of the fug as the grizzled old head of his dad's old friend Harry Thomas. Confused as to how Harry had appeared in this ghastly place, when he'd left him snoring on his bench, Turner desperately tried to make out what the old medic was trying to tell him.

'I'm done for Jakey – dying all over again old mate and, Christ it hurts like fuck, please help me...'

With that, and before Jake could offer comfort, the gasping stopped and Harry the Dog was no more…

Distraught, Jake continued his crawl through the depths of misery and presently discovered a small space of his own towards the back of the charnel house where he could gather his befuddled thoughts. He didn't know how long he'd been there, up against the wall in that dark abattoir, but smelling the sweet breath of one who was still very much alive, and feeling the warmth of it on his cheek, he opened his eyes. Through the tunnel, which had become his vision, Jake saw the welcome sight that was his daughter Sarah.

'Sarah, you came back' he rasped through dry, cracked lips.

'Sshh , Dad…' the girl went 'Sshh…'

With a colossal struggle, the girl's stricken father propped himself up and tried to take her hand in his but it just flopped uselessly into his lap.

'Forgive me Sarah…' he began. Tenderly taking his hand in hers, the girl put her mouth to his ear and spoke the words Jake had longed to hear.

'It's OK dad, I forgive you – I love you and I'm proud to be your daughter'

Weakly squeezing Sarah's hand, her absentee father fell back against the wall. He could see his daughter's lips moving in the gloom, but the noise in his ears prevented him from hearing anything. Suddenly, without warning his head felt as though it had been whacked full force by a demonic baseball bat, and he screamed a terrible unearthly scream, like that of a pig herded into the killing house and sensing too late, its violent fate. Through the blinding stars of pain bouncing around in his skull like some satanic pinball machine, his dying brain registered searing agony, first in his arm and leg and then moving cruelly as evil barbed spears, which thrusted relentlessly through his entire body. Once again, Jake Turner was immersed in the trauma, which had taken his life, now cruelly replayed from that fateful morning on the Victoria line platform back in the land of the living. With a death throe shudder, Sarah's dad was gone – erased like an old magnetic tape cassette, and nothingness – a word he'd often used back in the world to describe what being dead must surely be like – nothingness prevailed…

Sitting next to her father's broken body, an odd but sudden burning feeling in her neck, made Sarah Tunney flinch. She gasped involuntarily and her fingers flew to the source of her discomfort, the spot where her artery bulged thick with the blood of the living. She believed that she'd seen her own future and it terrified her. Kissing her father's cold forehead, she made her way through the miserable mass of the dead and the dying and reaching the door, heaved it open, before fleeing the horror of the charnel house and running towards the brightly lit corridor beyond…

POSTSCRIPT

Joe Small – driver of the Victoria line train, which had ended Jake Turner's life, went on to claim his right to retire under the "three and you're out" rule. The cop had been his third "victim" the previous two having been "jumpers" – that is to say – people who'd decided to commit suicide by tube train. It had been irrelevant, that Turner had been pushed against his will to his death, and at the age of 35, Joe Small had taken advantage of the rule, and retired to the rural surrounds of Hampshire on a pension, which, although handsome, had done little to compensate the recurring nightmares of smashed and bloodied faces pressed up against his windscreen.

Suleiman Muhibbi – Driver of SUL 1 attended the Old Bailey where Jake Turner had been summoned to give evidence against him in the case of the dismembered Turkish gangster. Upon hearing the tragic news of the prosecution's star witness's demise, His Honour Robert Masterson, had adjourned the hearing for a respectable period and to allow the Crown Prosecution Service time to regroup. Muhibbi was granted bail, with the condition that he sign on daily at his local police station, but fearing the jury's sympathy vote, he promptly absconded and flew to Northern Cyprus, from where there was no extradition treaty.

Mary Tunney – Mother of Sarah, despite the almost permanent anaesthesia of cheap cider, had been grief stricken by the news of her daughter's suicide. After the Scenes Of Crime Officers had made the briefest examination of Sarah's blood soaked and squalid flat, she'd been permitted to gather up the pathetic belongings accrued during her daughter's short life. She'd wept as she filled the bin liner with what little remained to mark Sarah's brief presence in the world, lingering briefly over the grubby Barbie doll that had once been her girl's only toy. Casting a rheumy eye over the bloody walls, Mary had left the flat and inexplicably walked the mile or so to her nearest church. There in the incense-laden air of the empty church, she'd lit a candle in memory of her daughter – the little girl she'd failed from day one of her short life on earth. Leaving the echoing place of worship, Mary Tunney had trudged around town in a trance and for the first time since she could remember, she'd gone through the entire day without a drink. As dusk fell, it found Sarah's mother sitting on a bench in the park, seemingly oblivious to the comings and goings of life around her. Pulling a crumpled card from her tattered handbag, she took out the cheap mobile phone from her coat pocket and dialled the number on the card.

Two days later, getting off the bus on the High Street, Mary Tunney walked down the alleyway which led to the community centre, and with a determination she'd not known since she'd ran away from home as an eleven year old, she climbed the creaking stairs to the second floor. Sitting down on the unyielding polyprop chair with the other men and women who shared her determination, she'd waited for her turn to come.

'Welcome Mary' beamed the rosy-cheeked woman at the front of the group. 'And what brings you here?'

Getting up, her chair legs scraping the linoleum floor, Mary, mother of Sarah, cleared her tobacco-ravaged throat.

'My name's Mary – and I'm an alcoholic…'

Phylida Parker-Jones – Seductress of Harry Thomas, had remained with her long- suffering husband; the one time Station Commander of RAF Luqa, and followed him into retirement from the service and his next job; that of British High Commissioner to South Africa. The couple had stayed together for appearances sake, and had pretty much led separate lives. So separate had their lives been, that Phylida had found other ways of satisfying the voracious sexual appetite, which had got her into trouble back on Hot Rock. Her indiscretions, long since ignored by her indifferent husband, continued unabated.

Flattered by the attentions of a young clerk at the embassy, the commissioner's randy wife had embarked upon a barely concealed affair with the clerk. Being a creature of the past and not really being up to speed with the scourge of AIDS; now endemic across the African continent, Phylida had been at it hammer and tongs with the embassy worker, who unbeknown to her had been bisexual and suffering from HIV. Infecting his British lover, he'd eventually come clean and "Posh Knickers" had spent the rest of her days popping so many pills, she practically rattled.

Elsie Jones – Mother to Damien, made her way, on a bright and blustery April day to France, and Pointe De Grave, at the northernmost point of the Medoc. She'd made the pilgrimage from her rainy English town to the head of the Gironde estuary to pay her respects - both to her father Ernie Bishop killed during the war - and her young son, who'd idolised Ernie and had died from a congenital heart defect. Pointe De Grave had been the place, where two months earlier, a memorial had been inaugurated to the memory of the Cockleshell Heroes and the ill-fated Operation *Frankton*. Just ten miles from where the memorial now stood, the brave men of the Royal Marines, had set off on their suicidal journey paddling their flimsy canoes up the estuary to Bordeaux harbour.

Standing in front of the monument, strands of grey hair blowing around from under her hat, Elsie took in its striking design. Looking like some mythical figure from ancient Greece, it had been carved from stone to represent a strange figure of half man, half cuttlefish, embracing the Bordeaux estuary. Closing her eyes, she reflected on the father she'd barely known and on her son Damien, both of whom, she'd been immensely proud to call family. Bowing her head, the old lady placed a wreath on the memorial, the inscription on which read: *"To my brave father Ernie and my son Damien; both struck down in their prime – gone, but never forgotten…"*

Ajit Devar – Mild mannered postmaster, was recognised in the New Year's Honours List, and made a Member of The British Empire. The only holder of the MBE in the small village of Wing; scene of the robbery in which he'd valiantly fought off the shotgun wielding thug from London, continued to improve his little shop and expanded his empire along the little High Street. With the help of an entrepreneurial nephew, the "Invincible One" went on to establish a successful restaurant, the main feature of which was the huge framed portrait depicting his meeting with the Queen at Buckingham Palace. Upon arrival, his guests, curious to meet the local hero, would be greeted with the sight of the postmaster holding up his medal and beaming proudly down at them.

Mickey Casey – Father of Michael, put up a hideous memorial to his son in the local cemetery. Looking akin to that of dead Russian gangsters, the oversized black marble headstone featured a full size

126

image of his son, dressed in hoodie and baggy jeans above crossed automatic handguns etched into the marble. Bizarrely, a string of rosary beads draped over hands clasped in prayer, also adorned the headstone in some grotesque pretence of piety. All in all, the whole tableau represented all that had gone wrong with British society. Rosaries worn around the necks of young criminals - who couldn't have recited a Hail Mary if you'd paid them – had become the trend, as had the ubiquitous two finger and thumb sign, pointed gun-like, which featured in pretty much every posed picture posted onto their Face book page. Wise to surveillance, but not put off by his stretch in The Scrubs, Casey senior continued to inhabit the criminal world, making sure to keep his hands clean and his house clear of incriminating contraband. Three years after his son's murder; tired and frustrated by the limitations on his criminality, he took up an offer and left the country, moving to what the British tabloids referred to as Spain's *Costa Del Crime*. There, among the fugitive armed robbers and fraudsters, he thrived, setting up a lucrative tobacco and alcohol smuggling ring which, took advantage of Spain's low tax duties. From his newly bought villa with its obligatory swimming pool, the crook from London, orchestrated the export of large quantities of booze and cigarettes to France and Britain, making a handsome profit in the low risk process.

62nd Infantry Regiment – Surrogate home to the Rupert, Pat and Jim, held a homecoming and medal presentation parade for what was left of the Battalion after the meat grinder that had been Helmand Province in Afghanistan. It was a beautiful summer's day and above the barracks, skylarks fluttered, their chirping calls so quintessentially British. To the sonorous beat of a solitary drum, the men marched onto the regimental square, heads held high and chests puffed with pride. Behind them hobbled the men on crutches, and to their rear, rolled the men in wheelchairs - the amputees and the paralysed - brave men refusing to yield to their injuries. Medals were awarded, speeches made and families cheered and waved Union Jacks.

Presentations over, speeches complete, the voice of the regimental adjutant rang out calling the assembled veterans to attention. A single thunderous crack of boots on tarmac represented discipline and a sense of total unity. The thunderclap startled the birds overhead, driving them away and silencing them. The officer's next command was to "Present Arms" and the parade square echoed to the rattle of two hundred rifles and the slap of calloused hands on the green plastic stocks of personal issue weapons. The same weapons toted during six months of dusty, energy sapping and lethal patrols into no man's land. The same rifles foolishly commissioned by the politicians in Whitehall, totally unfit for purpose and dogged by stoppages, poor quality and inadequate stopping power.

Leaving the soldiers at the present arms, the adjutant handed over proceedings to the regimental chaplain, who in time honoured tradition recited the fourth stanza from the poem by Laurence Binyon, composed on the East cliff above Portreath in Devon in 1914 for the fallen of another war – The Ode Of Remembrance "For The Fallen"

"They shall not grow old, as we that are left grow old:
Age shall not weary them, nor the years condemn
At the going down of the sun and in the morning,
We will remember them..."

The haunting, lilting melody of a lone bugler playing "The Last post" rang out; drowning out the male self-conscious mutterings of: "We will remember them" and as the last echoing notes died away, they were replaced once more by the sound of skylarks high in the sky. The adjutant gave the command to "Shoulder Arms" and the men of the 62nd once again manoeuvred their rifles about their bodies before returning them as one to the shoulder. Falling the men out, the adjutant led the way into the battalion restaurant for a buffet meal and drinks with family and loved ones. As for the families and friends without living heroes to congratulate; just shiny posthumous medals in presentation cases – the likes of the Rupert's brother, Jim's young daughter and Pat's mother – they were all drawn into the fold of the regimental family and regaled with the antics of their loved ones and stories of heroism. And there were gruff manly hugs for the bereaved, hugs given by the brothers in arms of the dead; wordless hugs that required no sound track, hugs that voicelessly said all there was to say and went further to dispel grief than any counselling group ever could. And then they dispersed, released from duty for two weeks leave. Two weeks in which to fuck, drink, fight, love and forget the horror that had been Helmand. And when they returned to the mundane barrack duties of peacetime soldiering; sentry duty at Buckingham Palace, painting, cleaning and the bullshit of parades, they'd know, that within a year, the adjutant – the same officer who'd handed out their medals – would muster them, bring them to attention once more and inform the young men of the 62nd of their next tour of Afghanistan...